# THE LAST DRAGON KIN

The Fallborn Series - Book 1

# T. L. RIFFEY

Publishing Coordinator – Sharon Kizziah-Holmes

Paperback-Press
an imprint of A & S Publishing
A & S Holmes, Inc.

ISBN -13: 978-1-951772-19-2

# DEDICATION

To dragon lovers everywhere.

# PROLOGUE

*B*eka Lane shifted behind her mistress as their mount changed its gait. She had never ridden a daggit before though she had taken care of them at the inn where her father had been in charge of the stable.

*Daggits were, according to her father, an unholy mix between a horse and a large dragon. Their basic body structure was like that of a horse, but it was a reptile, not a mammal, and some were even winged. The one they rode however was not, nor was it the normal gray-green, but a brown-green. Her mistress said it was called Warchild, and had been trained as a Warsteed; but why would a Messenger need a fighting Steed?*

*Warchild twitched his head and the messenger*

*pulled him up, then moved him off the road until they were looking back the way they had come. This was the third time they had left the road today. The last time two riders had raced by their hiding spot in a patch of wood, but here there was nothing but flat land around them..*

*"Mistress?"*

*"It'll be fine. Just be quiet."*

*"All right."*

*Why had her father sent Beka with the Messenger? Why leave in the middle of the night? Her mistress did not answer when she asked those questions, though she talked about her work readily enough the last three days. The last two evenings were spent talking around the campfire of the places her mistress had been and who she had met. Beka quite enjoyed those talks; they kept her from being too homesick. This was the first time in her seventeen years she had ever left her home village, and while it was exciting she missed her two younger brothers and father. Her eyes misted as she thought of the family she left behind.*

*Her brothers took after their father; long, lean, and blond as snow, but she took after their mother. Beka was moderately tall, but stout and mousy haired. Only her eyes were the same as theirs; gray. They all had a way with animals; mainly because they had been around them since the day they were born. Their father had been stable master at that inn for years before he had met and married their mother. What or who their mother had been before she married their father they never knew but she worked with their father afterward. Beka had been nine when their mother died, leaving their father to care for three children and care he did. All three of them were treated the same, taught the same, though Beka seemed to have a knack for learning.*

*"We should be at the inn within the hour," her mistress said, breaking into Beka's thoughts. "We'll be staying the night if all goes well."*

*It had been two days since they diverted from the main road onto this one, scarcely wider than a cart track. They'd seen little signs of habitation, only grassy hills with patches of forest here and there and a farmstead a few miles back. This track was used so there was some traffic here which usually meant a town or village that the farmer went to regularly.*

*A rider appeared on the road and Warchild pawed the ground. The rider slowly approached, then pulled his mount up before them.*

*"What a fortuitous meeting." The man gave her mistress a strange smile.*

*"Why do I doubt that?"*

*"We've been looking for you for a while, Messenger Penn."*

*"Well. You found me. Now what?" Her mistress shifted a bit.*

*The man made a move toward his belt, but before he could complete the move, he fell from the saddle.*

*Her mistress slid off Warchild and moved cautiously to the slumped form. Beka could see a knife in both her mistress' hand and sticking out of the man's chest. The hand without the knife touched the man's neck briefly before her mistress stepped away.*

*"Mistress?"*

*"Everything's fine, child." She slipped the knife in her hand back up her sleeve before she pulled the knife from the man's chest. "Come help me put him on his horse."*

*Beka obediently slid off of Warchild and they both managed to get the man on his horse. Her mistress used some rope she scavenged from his bed roll to tie him lightly to the saddle before slapping the horse's rump. As it took off across the field, she turned to Beka. "You're not to speak of this to anyone. You understand?"*

*"Speak of what, Mistress?"*

*"You're a good child." Her mistress patted her cheek. "Now let's get to that inn. I'm starving."*

*They both swung onto Warchild's back and he was pointed back to his original heading. Warchild paused at the top of the hill an hour later, allowing its two riders to look into the pseudo valley that spread out before them.*

*The village was small but seemed prosperous. They could see the inn; from here it looked well-built and had a large stable. It looked as if the village had been built around the inn which was common along more popular trails and caravan routes.*

*Warchild started down the hill, and her mistress sighed as if in relief.*

*"Mistress?"*

*"I told you to call me Calli, child," her mistress said, her dark eyes flashing under the hood of her cloak.*

"Yes, Mistress Calli."

Her mistress sighed. "What, Child?"

"We're near the border, aren't we?"

"Yes, about fifteen miles south of it to be exact." Calli waved a hand. "The land between us and Rennon was even called the Borderlands before the king of Rennon conquered it. Now only the Phenn River and a few mountains divide Eldan from Rennon."

"The tales are true?"

"Depends on the tales," Calli said. "I want you to stay with Warchild like you did at the other inn."

"Alright, Mistress." Beka remembered the crowd that had gathered around Warchild's stall, but which had dispersed when they caught sight of her in the stall. Daggits were not rare, but they were quite valuable. Ignorant people would no doubt think it would be easy to steal a daggit like they would a horse, but daggits were not horses and Warchild was war trained. One word from a handler and the thief would realize his/her folly. And Beka knew that word.

Her mistress patted Beka's pant-covered leg to get her full attention. "Don't spend too much time away from War. We may have to leave in a hurry."

"Should I eat in the stable then?"

"No," her mistress said after a moment's thought. "I don't want to draw too much of the wrong attention."

Beka didn't understand what she meant but didn't ask since they had entered the inn's courtyard and had an audience made up of the innkeeper and one of his stableman. Both had the *blond hair of native Eldanians, but the stableman's eyes were dark, showing he had Rennon blood. Her mistress helped her down, and Beka moved to Warchild's head to grip his bridle.*

*"Messenger." The innkeeper gave Calli a nod. "I am Cyrus the keeper of this humble inn. This is my head stableman Larek."*

*"Innkeeper. Larek." Calli returned the nod before dismounting. "I need a room for myself and a stall for my Steed and Beka."*

*The innkeeper's head jerked up as he stared at her mistress. "She's to stay with the steed?"*

*"Aye. Less of a fuss that way."*

*"Right." The innkeeper visually gathered himself. "If you'll follow me..."*

*"I'll see my steed settled first, then Beka and I'll eat before you show me my room. I might have to leave."*

*The innkeeper nodded and gestured to the stableman. "Then Larek will take care of you while I set you up a table."*

*"Good." Her mistress turned to Larek with a gesture. "Lead on."*

*Beka followed the stableman with her mistress at Warchild's shoulder. Larek lead them to the first stall that was empty and left to get food for the daggit without a word. Calli unlatched her pack and swung it onto her shoulder while Beka checked the riding straps and girth. The stableman returned as Beka finished checking the bit-less bridle, and Beka helped him settle the daggit in the stall. Since they might have to leave in a hurry, the saddle remained on the Steed.*

*After Warchild was comfortable, Beka moved to her mistress' side and followed her into the inn.*

*The dark stone-walled common room of the inn was much cooler than the courtyard outside. An empty table awaited them in a shadowy corner with a platter of food, and they moved quickly to it as their stomachs growled. Cyrus brought a pitcher of ale for Calli and a mug of water for Beka, and then left without a word so they could eat. Her mistress ate fast, but neatly, her eyes no doubt roaming the room. Seven other people shared the room and anyone of them could be the one that Beka's mistress was waiting for.*

*"Beka."*

*"Yes, Mistress?"*

*"Your father ever tell you about the Kellian Forest?"*

*"He showed it to us on the map in the inn and told us that was where both our grandmothers were from. Our paternal grandmother told tales of her childhood there with her Forester father. Da didn't say much about our maternal grandmother though."*

*"I suppose he wouldn't," her mistress said.*

*"My brothers would hear talk sometimes in the inn when they helped clean up at night from some of the travelers. They'd tell me about it but none of us believed most of it."*

*"A wise decision." Her mistress poured herself another mug of ale. "Remember don't wander tonight."*

*"I won't. Goodnight, mistress."*

*"Goodnight, child."*

*Beka slid out of the chair and headed out the door. She decided to visit the privy before settling in the stall with Warchild. Many a night she had spent in a stall at her father's inn so it would be no hardship to sleep with the Warsteed. The nights were getting cool; it would soon be autumn and sleeping with either a warm-blooded animal or fire-blooded reptiles was better than a blanket anytime in her mind. She took care of business in the privy and moved toward the stable, her mind already on sleep.*

*A step in the stable and she paused, her eyes registering the two blond men standing by Warchild's stall. The Warsteed was eyeing the strangers and pawing the ground, his claws sheathed for now. His topaz eyes flickered to her then went back to the men as she moved forward.*

*"Gentlemen." They were obviously not stablemen by both the better cut and style of their clothes so she gave them the generic title for citizens. "May I help you with something?"*

*"Whose mount is this?" the one on the left demanded.*

*"Messenger Calli Penn" Beka slid carefully past them and into the stall, her hand moving to rest on the Warsteed's shoulder.*

*"A Messenger..." The one on the right stepped back with a glance at his companion.*

*He gave an off-handed wave. "Doesn't matter...Girl, tell her I've claimed him."*

*"And who might you be?" came her mistress' voice as she stepped into view.*

*The man drew himself up. "I'm Lord Ivery's son,*

*that's all you need to know, woman."*

*"I'll need more than that to put on your tombstone, boy," Calli said, still standing in the doorway.*

*"I have the right to claim anything in this land, woman, and I claim this daggit. He's wasted on you anyway."*

*Beka moved to give the daggit room as it shifted but stayed where she could see what happened. Her mistress was still by the door and her voice was still calm, but Beka could see the tension in her mistress' form.*

*"The Queen gave me that daggit, boy. A queen outweighs a lord's brat any day."*

*"I'm taking him, woman, and if you try and stop me, I'll use more than my sword on you." The man made a grab for Warchild's bridle, but ended up on the floor. The daggit laid a claw on the man's back, holding him prone easily. "You're dead, woman."*

*"I didn't touch you, boy. If you knew anything about daggits, you'd know better than to try and steal one."*

*"I claimed him!"*

*"Call it what you will, it's still stealing. I'd advise you to learn more about daggits and to read your laws more thoroughly about claiming. Now my friend's going to let you up. I'd further advise you to leave him alone. He has your scent now and he doesn't forget." Her mistress made a gesture and Warchild removed his claw from the man's back. As he got to his feet, Calli moved away from the door. "Goodnight, gentlemen."*

*The other man dragged the Lord's son away and*

out the door before the man could say anything. Her mistress chuckled and moved to the stall, her hand gesturing in a calming motion. "It's okay now, old friend."

Snorting, the daggit stretched out his head. Calli patted Warchild's neck firmly while the daggit calmed.

"Was there something you needed, Mistress?" Beka asked.

"Just a meeting place, child," her mistress said as a shadow entered the stable and hovered. Calli gave the daggit one last pat and moved to where the shadow stood. It was obviously someone using a bit of sight-bending.

Beka moved to the rear of the stall and made a bed for herself with some of the hay she and the stableman had used earlier. When the daggit was ready it would settle next to her and rest while she slept.

A thump made her look up and she was staring at a quivering arrow stuck in the wall by her head. Warchild screamed, and Beka heard a heavy thud which shook the floor. Glancing toward the daggit, she saw a body laying at the entrance to the stall, and Warchild was lashing out with his front claws. A human scream denoted a hit, and then her mistress was pushing past the daggit.

"Come here, child." Calli was leaning against Warchild, her cloak torn and bloody. "I need your help."

Beka hurried to her mistress' side, but when she moved to help her, the woman grabbed her hand. "None of that, child. Get up on War."

*"But…"*

*"We haven't got time, child." Her mistress almost threw her onto Warchild's back. She reached into her cloak and drew out a small hand-sized chest, giving it to Beka. "Stick that into your tunic, child."*

*Obeying, Beka settled the box in her breast-band. "Mistress…"*

*"No time, child…Now head to the Killian Forest."*

*"Mistress…"*

*"I said we have no time. The others will be here soon." Calli slipped her cloak off and handed it to Beka. "Put this on and get going."*

*Beka stared at the wound in her mistress' shoulder as she absently took the cloak.*

*Before she could say anything, Calli made a gesture and Warchild took off at a run. Beka tightened her legs to keep from sliding off and Warchild quickened his pace. Turning her head, Beka caught sight of riders entering the courtyard behind her, and she quickly leaned into Warchild's pace. She slid the cloak on, and felt a shimmer as it settled over her shoulders.*

*The noise behind her grew louder, but she did not turn to look.*

# CHAPTER I

The sun was approaching zenith by the time Beka Lane reached the edge of the Killian Forest. They had been traveling west from dawn to dusk for the past three days, both to get to the forest and to keep ahead of the riders that were no doubt following them from the inn. Warchild seemed to be following some hidden trail of his own since Mistress Penn had sent them away because Beka had had no idea how to get to the forest. The sight of the forest was a relief to Beka since it meant the end of the ride was near, though where Mistress Penn had meant them to go here in the forest was still a mystery.

Leaves and branches blocked the sun, causing the world to seem green tinged as they entered the forest proper. Warchild pushed through some bushes, and Beka realized they were following some kind of trail that was winding off the main track deeper into the forest. The trees in the small patch of forest near her small village were nowhere as tall, nor as big, as the trees that surrounded her. Her paternal grandmother had told her about the forest where she had lived as a child, but Beka had always believed they were just bedtime tales, stories to entertain little ones. The truth of those tales surrounded her now.

Warchild pulled up and danced sideways, his head flickering to the left. Beka immediately searched the en-shadowed treeline, almost missing the raggedly dressed man who stepped forward at her movement. He carried a rough looking bow, an arrow notched, but not yet pointed at her.

"Messenger." The voice was as harsh as the face it came from. Scars lined the face and the eyes were as cold as the steel they resembled. "Why are you here, Messenger?"

"Calli Penn sent me," Beka answered truthfully. Warchild was not acting as if he sensed danger from this man so Beka decided to see if he was who her mistress had meant for her to go to. The arrow would not penetrate Warchild's hide, and the man would be dead seconds later.

"Warchild gave that away, Messenger." The man paused as his eyes settled on the soiled cloak she wore again. "Where is Messenger Penn?"

"I don't know. We were attacked and she sent me here."

"Attacked? Where?" There was a strange

urgency in his voice.

"At the Dreg Inn…"

"Strife!" the man cursed. "All was for naught then!"

Beka looked at the man for a moment, and then hesitantly retrieved the small chest from her tunic. "Perhaps not."

The man took a step forward before he controlled himself, his eyes on the chest. He let out a piercing whistle, and moments later another man stepped to his side. "Take over here. I'm taking the Messenger to the meeting place."

Beka had slipped the small chest back into her tunic as soon as the man had whistled. She may have decided to trust this man but others were still to be wary of. Warchild shifted under her, and she shifted her own leg, signaling him that it was alright.

"Messenger, if you'll follow me." The man gestured for her to follow as he slipped into the bushes lining the path.

Warchild obediently followed the man into the bushes at Beka's signal.

"What's your name, Messenger?" the man asked over his shoulder.

"Beka Lane. And you, guard, what's your name?"

"Ley Pierce, Messenger. Most call me Pierce."

"What is this meeting place we are heading for? Who's there?"

"Right now just a small group, but as soon as it gets dark enough some of Warchild's winged brethren will be flying in some potential Eldanian allies."

"So you are rebels from Rennon."

"I guess you could say that," Pierce said with a side glance.

A flicker of Warchild's head preceded the appearance of another sentry by a few seconds, and Beka watched as Pierce greeted him. Pierce whispered a few words, and the sentry faded back into the forest. Warchild moved forward at Beka's signal and continued to follow the guard toward the meeting place. Seconds later they entered a small clearing draped in netting among the trees, no doubt concealing it from flyers.

Pierce headed for the large tent that occupied the center of the clearing, bypassing the fire pit and the cook standing next to its kettle. Beka watched as Pierce entered the tent, but she remained on Warchild's back, her eyes flickering between the cook and the tent entrance.

A man appeared in the entrance with Pierce at his back, and Beka frowned. His hair was as mousey as hers and his facial structure was familiar. He was dressed in leather like a soldier, but only carried a short sword. She kneed Warchild forward, and stopped him before the tent, her eyes still on the man.

"Messenger, Pierce tells me you have news of Messenger Penn." His voice was tired as were his storm-gray eyes.

"Yes."

"Please come inside and tell me the tale if you would."

Beka slid off Warchild's back and gave him the

signal to stay. As the man turned to reenter the tent, she reached out and touched his arm. "Before we talk, I want to ask you something."

"Alright, Messenger. Ask."

"Are you related to Mercy Shallan?"

The man blinked. "Where did you hear that name, Messenger?"

"From my mother."

"Mercy was my youngest sister. She left almost twenty years ago instead of marrying a man she didn't love."

"Well, then I have more than one tale to tell you."

Keth Shallan, leader of the rebels, looked at the Messenger standing before him. "Perhaps you do," he said as he led the way into the tent.

Beka paused just inside the entrance, her eyes going to the table and chairs set up in the center of the tent. When Shallan gestured to a chair, she moved to the nearest one, but did not sit. "I've been in the saddle since dawn so I think I'll stand a while."

"Alright." Keth sat in the chair at the head of the small table. He made a gesture and Pierce left the tent. "Why don't we start with what happened with Messenger Penn."

With a nod, Beka launched into the tale of what happened since she and her mistress had got to Dreg Inn. Pierce entered half way through with a pitcher and two mugs which he set on the table between them before standing quietly behind Keth. When Beka got to the point of when Warchild had left the courtyard, Pierce cleared his throat, and Keth held up his hand to stop Beka's tale.

"Then you didn't see what happened to Messenger Penn?" Pierce asked.

"No." Beka shook her head.

When Pierce remained silent, Keth spoke. "What interests me is the one who tried to take Warchild. You say he said he was Lord Ivery's son?"

"Yes."

"But he didn't say which one?"

"No."

"Hmmm." Keth exchanged a look with Pierce. "I also find it interesting how soon the invaders showed up after the exchange. Did you see any sign of pursuit?"

"No."

"I think I'll just go have a chat with the sentries," Pierce said, slipping out of the tent as Keth nodded.

"For right now," Keth told Beka, "I think you should hold onto that chest for me until we get back to our main camp. Not that I don't trust my own men here, but-"

A roar from outside interrupted his words, Beka rushed to the tent's entrance. She paused briefly at what—who she saw, then moved to grab Warchild's bridle. The two men she had last seen in the Dreg inn's stables were standing before the tent, their faces visible in the dim light of early evening.

"You!"

"What are you doing here, girl?"

"Keeping Warchild from killing you at the moment," she snapped back at the irritated tone the Lord's son used.

"Kerr Ivery, you are early," Keth said from the

tent's entry before the Lord's son could speak. "It is not yet dusk."

Kerr Ivery waved his hand. "Why waste time with nonsense?"

"Nonsense," Keth echoed in a calm voice as he made a small gesture. Beka noticed the cook slipping away into the forest as Keth shook his head at Kerr. "Where is your guide, Ivery? How did you get past the sentries?"

"Ah, found me out did you." Kerr laid a hand on the hilt of his short sword. "No doubt the girl told you about what happened at the inn."

"How much are lives worth these days?" Keth asked, his own hand on his sword.

Before Kerr could reply an arrow struck the tent by Keth's head and he dropped to the ground, rolling. Beka swung onto Warchild's back as both men moved to follow Keth, keeping her body as close to the daggit's as possible. Warchild reared and struck Kerr's companion, knocking him to the ground unconscious.

With a twitch of the reins, Warchild shoved Kerr with his shoulder, and Beka kicked him in the chest for good measure as they headed for the trees. Just as they entered the trees, an arrow struck Beka between the shoulder blades and nearly knocking her from the saddle. She managed to stay on and tightened her legs, barely holding onto consciousness as pain shot through her.

Warchild suddenly stopped, and Beka swayed in the saddle. A hand touched her leg and she raised her head to see Pierce standing next to Warchild. He turned to look at someone behind him, and then swung up onto Warchild's back with her. She felt a tugging on her back, and heard a crack, pain shooting briefly between her shoulders. Pierce wrapped an arm around her waist, holding her, and then tapped Warchild's side.

"It's bad," Pierce was saying, obviously answering someone. "There's blood in front too."

"Crack his hide!" That was Keth's voice.

Beka just drifted along, listening to the two talk. The less she moved, the less the pain, although she was feeling a warmth spreading in her chest. It didn't feel like the blood spreading down her back; this was definitely a separate feeling.

"If we had just brought a Healer along," Keth was saying.

"Still wouldn't do us any good right now," Pierce replied. "Even if the others had escaped they're not here."

"How'd he even know about Messenger Penn?"

"Calli's sympathies were well known."

"Strife!" Keth cursed. "I find out I have a niece I didn't know about, I have the Gem within my grasp, and then I lose almost everything because of that crackhide!"

Beka's hand fumbles with her tunic, but Pierce grabs it and holds it still. "It's all right where it is, girl. Don't be moving about so much right now."

A hand ruffles her hair. "It's okay. I'm just rumbling, Beka. You just rest for a while."

"I can't," she mumbles. "It won't let me."

The hand on her head pauses. "What won't let you?"

The heartbeat, she wants to say. It was pounding

in her chest alongside her weaker one, not allowing her to rest. She shook her head weakly, but doesn't speak.

Pierce's hand at her waist shifted, his fingers spreading out. Warchild stopped, and Beka could almost feel Pierce's surprise. "I feel two heartbeats."

"What?"

"There are two heartbeats," Pierce repeated. "One is weak, barely there, but the other is very strong."

There was silence for the moment, and then Keth said, "The prophecy mentioned two hearts beating as one…"

"They are not beating together," Pierce said. "And the one, hers no doubt, is barely there."

Beka's hand fumbled with her tunic again, but this time Pierce didn't try to stop her movements. She drew out the small blood-soaked chest and carefully opened it, withdrawing the hand-sized Gem within. It was glowing with emerald fire like all dragon Gems, though this one pulsed like a heartbeat. Beka allowed the now useless chest to fall to the ground as she pressed the gem against her breastbone, and nearly screamed, pain shooting through her. She slumped forward, her arms going limp as she gasped for breath. .

Pierce's hand shifted again as he kept her in the saddle.

"There's only one heartbeat now." he said after a moment.

"The arrow is still in her back though," Keth said.

"I wish you'd stop talking as if I wasn't here," Beka said, still slumped over.

Before either could speak again, Warchild rumbled. Beka could feel Pierce shift even as she heard a repetition of the sound that had alerted the Warsteed in the first place; a soft rustling—as if something large was threading its way through the bushes around them. Pierce tensed, then relaxed against her, as he murmured, "Forester."

"We have an injured person, Forester. Is there a Healer nearby?" Keth's voice came from her left this time as if he had moved to protect them.

"There's a Caravan at the edge of the forest heading toward Lawr," came a gravelly woman's voice. "They usually employ a Healer."

"Can you lead us there by your short-cuts, Forester?" Keth sounded further away now. "The Messenger is sorely injured."

The Forester must have nodded because Warchild started to move again. Beka's back was numb, as if it had been rubbed with that salve that the Healer's used when they stitched a wound. She was grateful for that since if it wasn't she would no doubt be screaming and she didn't have the energy even for that. The darkness of unconsciousness was pulling at her, but she didn't want to go just yet. Why had she opened the chest, what had that Gem done to her, what...

"It's called the Dragon's Heart," Pierce's voice murmured in her ear.

Dragon's Heart; another tale her mother had told her as a babe.

"The Caravan is just ahead through those trees,"

came the Forester's voice. "I can take you no further."

"Thank you, Forester. May the Great Tree keep you safe," Keth told her. There was a rustle, and then Keth's voice came from beside Warchild. "Say nothing of either the Gem or why we were attacked."

"Aye." Pierce shifted, and Warchild slowed.

"Beka, just leave the talking to us, all right?" Keth spoke in her ear, before his voice raised, "Ho, in the camp, we have an injured Messenger."

"Enter in peace, travelers," came a man's voice.

There were other voices and sounds of animals, but Beka paid no attention to them; her back was starting to hurt again.

Warchild slowed to a stop, and Beka felt Pierce shift. Hands touched her and she loosened her legs, allowing them to pull her from the saddle. She was laid on her side, feeling a small pair of hands on her back, testing the area around the arrow shaft. Her eyes slid the rest of the way down, and the harsh yelling of a woman was the last thing she heard, as darkness swept over her.

# CHAPTER II

Warmth was the first thing Beka was aware of when she woke. Pierce was slumped against her cot, and beyond him Keth lay on a pallet asleep. They were in a small tent, and by the small amount of light that was coming through the tent opening it was still morning. Faint noises came coming from outside, but before she could recognize any of them, a small woman entered the tent.

"Ah, you've awakened." The woman moved past Keth who was showing signs of waking. She touched Pierce's shoulder, startling him awake. "I need some room, Mea."

Pierce noticed that Beka was awake and hurriedly stood, making room for the Healer. Beka watched him move to Keth, before she met the Healer's eyes.

"You no doubt have a lot of questions, me girl," the Healer said, looking carefully into Beka's eyes. "But you need to answer mine first, yes?"

"Okay," Beka said, her word slurred, but understandable.

"Good." The Healer leaned over Beka and prodded between her shoulder blades. "Any pain?"

"No. Heavy feeling. Hungry," she added as her stomach growled.

"That's the pain drug working then. After I pulled the shaft out, I used a bit of mind-healing on you, me girl. That's why you're hungry."

"She okay?" Keth asked, sitting up on the pallet watching the Healer.

"Yes. The wound's got to finish healing at its own pace, but she's no longer in danger."

"Good," Keth and Pierce both said together, making the Healer laugh.

"Now, the Caravan's heading out. We waited til now because I wanted to be sure she was well on the way to healing before we left. The Caravan's leader left you a mule for the tent and the bag of supplies he gave you outside. That should get you by for awhile. Just make sure she stays propped when she sleeps for a bit longer, and I included a bag of Caro tea for any aches or pains she may have in the supplies."

"Thank you again, Healer," Keth said as Pierce moved back towards Beka's cot.

"My pleasure as well as my duty, sir," the Healer replied as she turned toward the tent opening. "Just keep her safe; don't want all my work to go to waste."

"I'll do my best," Keth told her soberly.

"See that you do." The Healer gave him a nod, and then disappeared out the tent opening.

"I need to talk to Beka alone for a moment, if you don't mind, Pierce."

Pierce patted Beka's shoulder, and then disappeared out the tent opening himself as Keth moved to Beka's cot. Keth settled on the floor next to her and leaned an arm on the cot. "How much did Mercy tell you about us?"

"Not much." Beka's voice was still slurred, but clear. "She told me tales of when she was a child."

"Ah," Keth paused. "Father was a harsh taskmaster. I was twenty when Mercy left."

"She had a good life with Da," Beka told him. "He's the stable master at Des Inn."

"Had?"

"She died of a fever nine years ago. The Healer couldn't help her."

"Do you have any siblings?"

"Two younger brothers. I had an older sister, but she died of the same fever that took Ma."

"Do they look like you, these brothers?"

"No." Beka shook her head. "They take after Da so did Sali."

Keth's free hand moved to brush the bangs from Beka's forehead as he stared at her for a moment. "Did she tell you the tales of the Dragon's Heart?"

"Tales? She only told me about the girl that stumbled upon a Gem and found out that it was the heart of a dragon. When an evil man tried to steal it, the gem reduced him to ash.”

“That’s the tale Grandfather told us about the prophecy. So she didn’t tell you specifics?”

“No.”

“Hmmm.” Keth touched Beka’s temple, his eyes thoughtful. “Dragons were plentiful at one time, much like the daggits. Men like Kerr Ivery enslaved many of them for their elemental powers, causing them to seek death. Soon only a few dragons remained, mainly in the Borderlands where they were treated with respect. Then treachery was done and all but one dragon was destroyed making way for the King of Rennon to conquer the Borderlands. He kept the last Dragon’s Heart in one of his main temples to show everyone his power.”

“That’s not what the history books I’ve seen say happened.”

“History is written by the winners,” Pierce said as he entered the tent, carrying a large pack. “We saved a bit of breakfast for you. I’ll warm it up a bit then bring it as well as some tea for us.”

Keth nodded to him and waited until he exited the tent before continuing. “So there the Gem stayed for over a hundred years until a raid by some very stupid bandits. The Gem has been lost for thirty years until Messenger Penn told me she had heard of a rumor last year. She’s been hunting it down ever since.”

“So the meeting at the Dreg Inn was with one of her informants?”

“One of mine, you should say.” Keth gave a tired sigh. “I’m the leader of the rebels that have been attacking the military in what used to be the

Borderlands.”

“I realized that,” Beka told him with a faint smile. “From what little Pierce said on the way to the meeting place. Ma said that her family had been nobility at one time. I thought that meant they had been disgraced and that was why she didn’t want to talk about them.”

With a snort, Keth rubbed his one temple. “Not disgraced, displaced. So she never told you exactly what the Dragon’s Heart was or what it did?”

“No. Just that tale of the girl finding a Dragon’s Gem.”

Before Keth could speak, Pierce appeared in the tent opening. “Breakfast.”

Keth got to his feet, and pulled the blanket back from Beka. “The Healer said you should sit up a bit today.”

As Keth was speaking, Pierce came over to the cot and carefully removed one of the pillows behind Beka’s back that kept the pressure off her wound. Keth slipped his arm under her neck while Pierce slipped one under her side. Carefully, both men set Beka upright, holding her steady as she swayed.

“I’ll get the food,” Keth said, moving toward the tent opening.

“You got animal mind-speech, don’t you?” Beka asked Pierce. “That’s why Warchild likes you.”

“Well, partially,” Pierce allowed. “But mainly cause Calli’s my wife.”

Beka jerked her head up, nearly smacking Pierce in the face.

Pierce gave her a crooked smile. “I helped her train Warchild. I am a Master trainer at a school. I knew she'd be getting into some scrapes so I wanted to make sure she could get out of them."

Keth entered with a bowl and a mug and handed them to Beka, ending the conversation for awhile as Pierce left to get the tea. When he returned, both he and Keth settled with their mugs beside the cot. Beka took a few bites of the porridge before looking at Pierce, remaining silent even when Keth entered.

"I gather you told her Calli was your wife," Keth commented.

"Yes." Pierce set his bowl down. "I gather your sister didn't tell much about either the family or the Gem."

"I don't blame her about the family bit," Keth said, sipping from his mug.

"You're talking like I'm not here again," Beka told them both.

"Well, eat your porridge, and I'll tell you about Dragon's Heart, all right?" Keth retorted.

"Okay." Beka stirred the porridge and took a bite. "Go on."

"Right." Keth took a sip of his tea. "Did you know that dragons have two hearts?"

Beka shook her head, silently.

"The one is a flesh and blood heart, works just like ours pumping their blood. The second heart is what allows the dragon to control its elemental power. It's also how humans can enslave them. Though there were those called Dragon Kin who were companions to the dragons."

"That Gem was really a dragon's heart just like in the story?"

"Yes."

"And now it's a part of you." Pierce added

"Not much is known about how it controls the elemental power. The only thing known about how it actually combines with its 'host' is that it attaches to the soul. What is known for sure is what it does once merged." Keth continued "The dragon whose heart it comes from, is bonded to the human who bears it until one of them dies."

"So when the human dies of old age…"

"The human won't die of old age," Pierce interrupted her. "But lives as long as the dragon does. He's talking about other factors that would cause death."

"Like an arrow through the back?" she spoke softly.

"Yes." Pierce took her now empty bowl and stood. "I'll take care of this."

Keth gave him a nod as Pierce moved toward the tent entrance. "The Heart gives good health, speeds healing, and slows the aging, but it doesn't make one immortal. Dragons are mortal, just long-living ones."

"But the tales of dragons being around for several millennium…"

"Are mostly just that, tales; though they do enter a deep sleep sometimes that can last centuries. That's when humans can steal their second hearts and how the one you carry was taken. The dragon had entered its first such sleep and an evil man stole the heart, causing the dragon to remain in its sleep all this time."

"This Heart has never been—merged before?"

"No or the dragon—as well as the Gem—would

have been gone. And as of last year the dragon was still resting in its cave…"

"So the dragon should now be waking since I…"

"Yes. And he'll be searching for you."

"He? And what do you mean by 'searching for'?"

"According to the tales the dragon is a male, but Mercy and I always toyed with the idea that dragons were hermaphrodites. All the tales were of male dragons, never females." Keth shook his head. "And as for the 'searching for', that's exactly what I mean. He'll wake up and come for you. You have his other heart; you're his control."

"Control?"

"His elemental power. You know that we humans, some of us anyway, have mind-powers like telepathy, animal mind-speech, telekinesis and the like?" Keth paused as Beka nodded. "Well, dragons have other powers."

"Magic?"

"There's no such thing as true magic. Dragons use natural energy as well as mind-powers. They have control over an element--Air, earth, water, or fire. Some even have all four."

"So fire breathing dragons..."

"Have control--complete control over that element."

"What do you mean complete control?"

"Just what I said. The dragons can make their element dance to their will."

"Time for a nap," Pierce said as he entered the tent. "The healer said she must rest."

"But…"

"You don't have to sleep, child." Pierce moved to her side. "Just rest. Now let's lay you down."

Keth stood and helped Pierce lay her on her side. Pierce settled the pillows at her back, while Keth pulled up the blanket. Both men patted her arm when they were done, and moved to leave.

Beka reached out and touched Keth's arm. "Wait."

Pierce continued out as Keth turned to look at Beka. "Yes?"

"When are we leaving here? I know we have to get moving before the ones that attacked the camp find us."

"We'll leave at dawn tomorrow. Don't worry."

Beka watched Keth leave then closed her eyes, settling into the cot. She didn't think she'd be able to sleep with everything whirling in her head, but she'd at least give it a try. Her brain kept thinking about what Keth had said about mind-powers.

Only a few out of a hundred humans had any type of usable mind-power, and it was of varying degree, yet it was getting more common each decade. Empathy and to a slightly lesser degree mind-speech was the most common, then came the Healers. Their mind-power was a mixture of telepathy—or empathy, telekinesis, and something that still had no name; all three had to be present for a Healer to be able to work their 'magic'. Animal mind-speech was common among farmers, horse breeders and animal trainers of high standing as it was what made them the best. Others had lesser known mind-powers like sight-bending which caused the eye to blur over something or telekinesis.

What the dragons were said to be able to do, was much different, almost magical. Humans used their own energy to fuel their powers, though they could store energy in gems to do greater works. Dragons however could do things on a grander scale than humans.

When her first brother was born, Beka's mother had started telling the baby dragon stories, and Beka had enjoyed them as well while she played at her mother's knees. The stories got more elaborate as the baby got older, and by the time the second boy was born, her mother was telling the stories as if both were near grown and not littles. Each story was more spectacular than the last, and Beka never really believed them. Lightening called down from the sky, sandstorms on a calm day, or water spouts appearing in still waters just didn't seem possible. Flaming dragons were much more believable.

And this prophecy he mentioned? Keth hadn't told her anything about it, almost as if he wanted her to forget he mentioned it at all. At lunch she'd get him to tell her about it.

"I saw signs of recent travel on the road when I went to fill the bucket earlier," came Pierce's voice faintly from outside.

"Besides the Caravan's?" came Keth's soft rumble.

"Yes, fast horses."

"Running ahead…" Keth's voice faded as if he seemed to move away from the tent.

Or perhaps not.

Beka shifted her pillow under her head, her eyes now open and staring at the opposite end of the tent.

Were the fast horses the ones that attacked the meeting place? Were the attackers on their trail? Was Mistress Penn still alive and captive or had they finished what the others had started?

She was still pondering this when Pierce entered the tent. He silently shook his head and moved to stand before her cot. "Did you rest at all?"

"You said I didn't have to sleep," she told him.

"True. I'm starting lunch soon. Since you ain't sleeping, I'll send in Keth to keep you company."

"Good. I got questions."

"I'm sure you do." Pierce shook his head again and moved back towards the tent opening. "At least you should sleep tonight if you don't nap."

Keth actually passed him in the tent opening. "Didn't sleep?"

"Too much to think about," Beka told him as he moved to sit by the cot.

"In what order?"

"Stories Ma told my brothers about what dragons could do, what the Gem did to me, then what happened to Mistress Penn."

"I can see where that could keep you awake." Keth settled, leaning against the cot. "What do you want to know first?"

"What the Gem did to me," she blurted out. "Am I changed?"

"Ah," Keth rubbed his temple. "You're still you, Beka. As I said before, it speeds healing, slows aging, and gives you good health, but it doesn't change you into something else. You're still human with all the same strengths and failings therein."

"The dragon can't take me over? Ma's tales told

of dragons that could overwhelm a human's mind and control that human's body…"

"Dragons can do that to any human without strong mental shields and even to some with them. Or so it's been told in the all the tales I've heard."

"Then it won't drive me insane or try to control me so that it has its freedom?"

"The Dragon has a vested interest in keeping you healthy both mentally and physically if it wants to continue living. From what I heard some dragons did kill themselves when they were 'enslaved', but mostly because of the type of 'master' they had. Many were men like Kerr Ivery, but there were some fair-minded men, self-centered but fair-minded all the same. The Year of Death was even linked to the death of dragons."

"The Year of Death?"

"Mercy didn't tell you that tale, I guess. Perhaps I'll tell you that one on the ride tomorrow."

"How do you and Ma know all these tales?"

"Grandfather wrote them down and used to read them to us as bedtime stories when we were littles. He didn't want them to ever be forgotten. Our family were the caretakers to many dragons in the past and part of our family still watches over the cave where the last dragon's been sleeping."

"If the cave's been watched, how did the Gem get stolen?" This had bothered her.

"The King killed the watchers. By the time the others were on his trail, the gem was in the Temple. It was decided to leave it there with eyes upon it."

"You had spies at the Temple?" She was surprised they had been able to get someone inside.

"Until the thieves came."

"What about this prophecy you mentioned?"

"I think I'll leave that for when we're at the main camp."

"Why?"

"You know the basics from the tale Mercy told you. The specifics can wait."

"I got the stew simmering," Pierce said from the tent opening. "They left us some journey bread. Do you want it warmed?"

"Did they leave any garlic butter?" Beka asked, licking her lips at the thought.

"Yes." Pierce smiled. "So warmed it is."

Keth shook his head as he watched Pierce leave. "I just don't get what you Eldanians like about garlic butter. Mother liked it too, but the rest of us never got the taste for it."

"Tell me about the family. Why'd Ma never mention anything but childhood things?"

"Father was a harsh man. The Rebellion was all he seemed to live for, and only Mother seemed to be able to distract him from it. When she died he just seemed to forget about us except as members of his rebellion. Mercy, as you no doubt know, was a sensitive person."

"In more than one way. She was empathic."

"She could have been a Healer," Keth replied. "But Father had other plans for her. Had Mother been alive, well, things would have been different. When Mercy ran away, Father had to change his plans, which worked better in the long run, for all of us."

"I guess it's a good thing I'll never meet him."

"Hopefully, you'll get to meet your uncles Wills and Jens as well as your Aunt Joyce. Your Aunt Merry died two years ago, but you'll probably see your two cousins."

"I have cousins."

"Yes," Keth laughed. "Three of them with two others on the way. Well, unless Joyce has twins, then it'll be three more."

"Pa was an only child, though he had several cousins."

"Lunch is served," Pierce said as he entered the tent with two mugs and a bowl. He set everything down and moved to the cot as Keth got to his feet. "So let's get her upright."

"I can sit up on my own," Beka said as she pushed up onto her elbow. "I'm not feeling any pain."

Keth touched Pierce's arm to keep him still. "Alright, try it then."

Beka swung her feet off the cot and carefully sat up. "See?"

"Good," Pierce grunted as he handed her the bowl and mug he had retrieved. "I'll get our bowls."

Accepting the other mug, Keth nodded, then settled by the cot again. "No twinges?"

"Nope. I guess that increased Healing is true." Beka retrieved the slice of journey bread from the top of the bowl, sitting the mug on the cot beside her. "We can leave before dawn tomorrow, I think, if we need to."

Pierce entered and gave Keth a bowl of stew before settling nearby with his own mug and bowl. Keth smiled when he noticed his own bowl did not have a slice of journey bread while Pierce's did.

They all dug into the stew, ignoring conversation for now.

# CHAPTER III

Voices woke Beka before dawn the next day.

A lantern was hanging by the tent opening where Keth and Pierce were talking in soft voices. Keth noticed that she was awake and raised a hand to stop Pierce from talking. "How are you feeling?"

"Well enough to leave," Beka replied as she carefully sat up, the blanket falling to the cot. "As long as we eat a bit before leaving."

"That we can do," Pierce said with a grin. "I got porridge on the fire."

Keth moved quickly to the cot and helped Beka to stand, steadying her when she swayed. "While you eat, Pierce and I will take down the tent and pack everything."

"Sounds good to me," she said with a grin. She allowed Keth to help her to the tent opening, her eyes taking in her surroundings.

The fire was smoldering before the tent with a small kettle over it while to the right Warchild, a horse, and a mule were loosely picketed just at the edge the firelight. Warchild and the horse were saddled and the mule was harnessed. Keth and Pierce must have been arguing about when to wake her.

Sleep had claimed her soon after lunch yesterday, even though she had wanted to talk more with Keth. She remembered eating supper but sleep had not long surrendered its hold and she had been reclaimed quickly.

Pierce passed her and Keth with the folded cot which he set by the mule, before heading back toward the tent. Keth settled her by the fire on a camp stool and handed her a bowl of the porridge from the kettle before he rejoined Pierce.

Beka watched the tent come down as she ate her porridge, her mind still half asleep. The tent and pallet joined the cot by the mule, and Beka set her bowl aside. She had eaten about half of it, but other body functions were clambering. Moving carefully, she stood and went to take care of business behind a tree while the other two packed the mule.

"Are you ready?" Pierce asked her when she returned as Keth moved to the fire.

"Whenever you are," she told him, moving to Warchild's side.

Keth rinsed out the kettle, using the water to put out the fire afterwards. He settled the warm kettle and stool on the mule, then moved to the horse, swinging onto its back. Pierce checked the fire again before moving to Warchild and helped Beka onto his back. Glancing around one last time, Pierce joined her in the saddle and nodded to Keth.

"Right." Keth headed back into the Forest with Warchild and the mule following him. "We're heading for one of our outposts nearer the border. I'm going to take us in a circular route, hopefully by-passing Kerr Ivery's men and any others."

"So full days in the saddle then," Beka commented. "For a while."

"Mostly." Keth set his horse to the track that ran parallel to the forest. "It all depends on how things go."

"You said you would tell me about the Year of Death on the ride."

"I said I might tell you about it," Keth told her, glancing back. "Were you always so inquisitive?"

"That's how one learns."

"True enough," Keth paused. "The Year of Death. So called by those of the Borderlands because of the multitude of deaths that happened during that time. It started out with the harshest ice storm the Borderlands had ever seen in its mountains, then continued with a drought in the spring. The summer brought a plague that killed man and beast alike, and with the drought continuing…well, many died."

"That's when some of the dragons died as well," Pierce commented from behind her.

"Some just went mad and killed themselves," Keth said. "Then just before fall, the King of

Rennon laid siege. Luckily, the Borderland's royal family had had enough warning of his coming so most of them escaped as well as some of the Nobility. But many people died that fall and winter as the siege continued until the next Spring when the King of Rennon took the capital. So that is why it's called the Year of Death, and most Borderlands people count time as before or after that Year. It's 138 ADY by that count."

"I thought you said something about betrayal causing the dragons to die."

"The plague was man-made."

"The King of Rennon?"

"So it's been said." Keth shook his head. "It seems very suspicious that the plague seemed to kill the men of fighting age and left children and the elderly weakened, yet alive. Natural diseases attack those groups as they are the most vulnerable. It also attacked the reptilian animals like daggits while leaving sheep and other farm animals untouched. Many have speculated that the death of the dragons was an accident, and that the King of Rennon had only meant to weaken them enough to enslave them for himself."

"But if he killed the dragons' bonded with the plague…"

"Some of the dragons that died were unbonded. But I see your point, as have others. That's why I said speculated since we will never know, but I believe he only meant to kill the ones already bonded. With a few dragons on his side he could have continued the push into Eldan."

"Why did he stop?"

"The remaining dragons. Though dying they used the last of their strength to decimate half his army so he wouldn't have been able to hold more land."

"Why didn't he bond with the Heart then?"

"Personally, I think he was afraid."

"Afraid? Afraid of what?"

"Of the same things you were. Of being taken over by the dragon."

"Which is also, I think, why he had the Temple take it in." Pierce added. "So no one else would take it and merge since it would mean excommunication with the Church."

"Especially since the main reason he gave for the invasion was a religious one," Keth agreed. "The main stay of the King of Rennon's power is the Church so…"

"Unlike us," Beka commented.

"Right. Unlike Eldanians or the Borderlands." Keth shifted in his saddle.

"Where one can worship who one wills, not what only the Church wills," Pierce added.

"Thank the Lords for that!"

"In more than one way." Pierce laughed.

The mounts paused at the crossroads that lay ahead of them. Keth glanced back at the forest behind them, then at the hilly grasslands ahead before taking the right fork. Warchild shook his head but followed Keth's horse, the mule following peacefully behind him.

"Why'd Warchild do that?"

Pierce gave a grin. "Cause he knows it's greens for him, not anything else this way. At least for a while. Daggits like variety in their diets as you know, including some meat now and then. Knowing Calli, he's probably not had any for some time. She dislikes hunting."

"I thought she was a Naturalist," Keth commented. "She's in the Circle at Yagos."

"She is, but she doesn't like 'extinguishing a life spark' as she calls it just for herself." Pierce shrugged. "I think that's why she became a Messenger in part."

"Mmm."

"Keth, can I ask you something?"

At the serious tone, Keth glanced back at her and slowed his horse's pace. "Of course."

"What's going to happen to me when we get to the outpost?"

"What do you mean?"

"Am I going to be a guest or a prisoner?"

Keth pulled up and turned to look at her. "Why would you be a prisoner?"

"Why wouldn't I be?" Beka pinched her nose between her eyes as her head began to ache dully. It felt as if something was running rough fingers though her brain, but she pushed that thought away and concentrated on her more current worry. "The sub-leaders of your rebel group would no doubt want to control the dragon."

"I'm sure they would," Keth told her, meeting her eyes. "But I have the final say."

"If I was a captive…"

"Dragons don't do hostage situations," Keth interrupted. "They'd either fry the hostage taker or take them over."

"And who says we'll tell them anything about the dragon?" Pierce added.

"So I'm Mistress Calli's apprentice?" Beka gave a soft sigh as the headache subsided as suddenly as it had appeared. "Or your niece?"

"Both." Keth held her eyes a moment longer, then started his horse down the way again. "Both."

"What about this prophecy?"

"What about it? Your life is your own. The Gods always give us a choice."

"The alternatives are usually bad," Beka insisted.

"I will do whatever's within my power to help you," Keth told her, causing Beka to relax against Pierce in the saddle. "I won't let you stand alone."

"Not all of the tales had a happy ending."

"The prophecy ends with the destruction of the evil man."

"So Ma just added the 'happy ever after'?"

"Our grandfather did." Keth paused. "Did Mercy teach you the ancient tongue?"

"The basics of the written, but we spoke it regularly when I was a child."

"Then I'll get you a copy of the original as well as the translation."

"Ma said the translation could change with the inflection."

"The Oracle spoke it in the ancient tongue first, then in the Trade tongue." Keth shook his head. "It seems most of those present didn't understand her when she spoke the ancient tongue. Fortunately her scribe wrote out both versions."

"Does the King of Rennon know of this prophecy?"

"He's heard the rumors I'm sure, but the true version?" Keth shook his head. "I doubt it or he would have been more diligent about finding the Gem."

"Ivery seemed pretty diligent."

"About the rebellion. Whether he was at the inn to collect the reward for members of the rebellion or if it was just coincidence we may never know. I don't think he or the King knew why Calli was really there."

"A man came upon us before the inn. She seemed to know why he was there." Beka paused. "She killed him."

Pierce tensed. "Did she mention a name?"

"No." She shook her head. "But I noticed the brand on the horse and on the saddle bag were the same."

"Not Ivery's then?" Keth asked.

"It was three overlapping ovals inside a square, not one oval inside a square."

"The Rennon royal horse breeder brand." Keth frowned, then looked at Pierce. "Dillion?"

"What did he look like?"

"Typical Rennon. He had a faint scar on his left cheek."

"Dillion," Pierce confirmed. "You said she killed him?"

"Knife through the heart."

"Poetic." Pierce paused. "Dallion won't be far behind."

"Hopefully, he won't meet up with Kerr Ivery and make a deal before we get her away."

"What are you two talking about?"

"Calli had been promised to marry the heir of the Rennon royal horse breeder family when she was born. Her family is a cadet branch of the Eldanian royal horse breeder clan." Pierce paused as he allowed Beka to absorb this. "Well, she ran away and eventually married me. The Rennon family were--upset and declared a feud on Calli."

"To be honest only the heir and his sons declared the feud," Keth said.

"So he married and had kids?"

"Yep. Three boys and two girls." Pierce shrugged. "But he never got over what he called a slight to his honor."

Now Beka wondered which had caused them to leave her father's inn that night: the jilted suitor or a Rennon spy.

"Enough of this negativeness." Keth straightened in his saddle. "Tell me what you remember about your mother."

# CHAPTER IV

It was the late afternoon of the second day that they entered the foothills and timberlands near what used to be the Borderlands. They had met no one during their ride, and had only seen signs of recent travel in the last day. Last night after setting up her cot, the two men had divided the night watch and the chores, leaving her with nothing to do but worry. Despite Keth's words, she was still worried about what would happen when they reached the rebel outpost.

"You've been quiet today which means you're worrying again." Keth glanced back at Beka. "How many times do we have to tell you that you don't need to worry?"

"I don't know…Why are we going to *this*

outpost?" Beka suddenly asked.

"I wondered when you would get to that question," Keth said with a faint grin.

"Well?"

"It's our home camp," Pierce answered her. "The school I train mounts at is near here just this side of the border."

Keth stopped his mount and slid to the ground, his eyes intent on the ground. He dropped the reins and moved to a nearby tree, squatting to study the disturbed earth. "Looks like someone came through here not too long ago."

"On foot or mounted?"

"Looks like someone on foot was being chased by both."

"Do you think it's safe enough for me to visit a tree?" Beka asked Keth. "I mean it's not urgent right now or anything."

His hand resting on the ground, Keth glanced around, then looked back at her. "Just keep close. I don't like that someone's been hunting."

"Okay," Beka agreed as she slid off Warchild. Slipping past Keth, she located a nearby bush and took care of business. She settled her clothing and stepped out from behind the bush, almost tripping over a body. It hadn't been there a few minutes ago nor did she see signs of anyone else around. She gave a whistle and within seconds Keth appeared.

"Well, what do we have here?" a strange voice said as a horse and three men pushed forward. The rider held a crossbow casually across his lap while the other three men simply settled their hands on their weapons. "Dying dogs do seek out their own kind."

"So I imagine you were the one responsible for that?" Keth spoke calmly to the rider as he pointed to the body and kept his own body in front of Beka's.

"Indeed. One of two spies. No doubt your compatriots." The rider's eyes ran over Beka and she shivered at the look in those cold eyes, making the rider smile. "While my men take care of you, I'll be taking good care of that girl."

Before Keth could say anything, Warchild appeared behind the horse, causing it to rear and throw its rider. Keth drew his weapon and attacked, even as Pierce began his own attack.

Beka stumbled back, falling over the body and landed on her butt. The rider loomed up beside her but fell to the side with a look of surprise, a small ax in his back. She scooted away from the bodies and glanced around for Keth and Pierce. Both men were busy with their opponents, and Warchild was taking care of the last attacker.

Another man was standing nearby, a small ax, like the one in the rider's back, in his hand. His long black hair was held back by a band made of the same woven material as his boots while on his body he wore only a pair of leather pants and twin bands across his chest which must have supported whatever weapon that poked over his right shoulder. Blood and dirt stained both his chest and right arm, yet Beka saw no wound to account for them.

"Beka," Keth said to catch her attention. He and Pierce had finished off their opponents and were now looking towards the dark-haired man.

"I'm fine. Thanks to him."

The man casually retrieved the small ax from the dead rider's back, his green-brown eyes never leaving Beka. A flicker of a dark emotion appeared in his eyes when Keth moved and Beka held up her hand to keep Keth still. She had felt that.

"Who are you?"

"You know who I am," the man told her. "But you can call me Hawk if you need a name."

"How did you find me? Not that I'm complaining mind you," she added quickly, glancing at the dead man lying on the ground between them.

"You called to me," the man who was not truly human anymore replied. "And I found this one nearby."

"I called to you?"

He moved to stand in front of her, his free hand lifting to tap her temple. "In here."

Keth shifted, causing the man to look at him. "You're the dragon."

"In a manner of speaking." He turned back to Beka, his fingers playing with her hair. "This one was dying and I needed a body…"

"You took him over?"

"He had already departed though his body was still fighting." He paused as he seemed to think over his words. "I healed the body and slipped in...They hunted him."

"He must have been the other spy they were talking about," Keth said, watching as the man kept playing with Beka's hair.

"Yes." The man stepped back from Beka and

turned slightly to look at Keth. "This one carried a message to one Keth Shallen which I believe is you."

"Do you know what it was?"

"No. It was the last thing on his mind though." He paused. "However, there seems to be a mobilization of troops and some seem to be looking for where my dragon body is now located since those near the more mountainous areas with caves have mobilized the most."

"Mmmm," Keth stared at the man. "I gather your 'dragon body' is safely hid?"

"It's not where they'll find it."

"Okay," Keth paused, before asking, "Are you coming with us?"

"That depends on you and him," the man said, nodding towards Pierce. "I won't be a slave or on display."

"How do you know she won't do that to you?" Pierce asked, watching the man closely.

"I've touched her mind as well as her heart; I *know* what kind of person she is."

Beka blinked, then blurted out, "The headache I had that day!"

"Yes." Green-brown eyes met gray eyes and held for a moment. "I make no apology for wanting to know my fate."

"My family has watched over your sleep. I see no reason not to continue," Keth said in the sudden silence. "Pierce?"

"I will say nothing." Pierce looked at the man. "I can promise no more."

"That is acceptable." The man gave a nod to

Pierce and Keth. "You'd best start calling me Hawk then."

"Dylan Hawk," Beka said. "You need two names after all."

The man met her eyes again with a raised eyebrow.

"Unless you're an 'unlearned barbarian'."

"I will be acting like one," the newly named Dylan Hawk said. "For the most part anyway."

They all headed back to the road and Keth retrieved his horse. They all mounted up except Hawk.

"I'll be able to keep up," he assured them when they all looked at him.

Keth gave a nod and nudged his mount into a walk with both Warchild and the mule following close behind. He tried to engage Hawk in conversation but the dragon-man ignored him and he soon stopped trying.

A sentry greeted them a mile further on.

"Milord," a man said as he seemed to appear out nowhere.

"Darin," Keth said with a relieved laugh as he pulled up his mount. "You nearly gave me a heart attack."

"Then I haven't lost my touch," laughed the older man, his gray eyes merry. "I see Warchild, but the miss there is not our beloved Messenger."

"It's a long story, Darin, but this miss, as you call her, is my niece and Calli's apprentice."

"Well, that surely is a long story." The older man gave Beka a good look over, before turning his attention to the patiently waiting Hawk. "And this one?"

"I'm her bodyguard," Hawk said, returning the man's look. "You can just call me Hawk."

Hawk had kept up with the mounts and seemed unwinded. Every time, Beka had glanced sideways, he had been striding easily next to Warchild. He had let his eyes silently wander their surroundings as they traveled and had not spoken until the guard appeared. It was obvious he refused to discuss his situation any further. At least for now.

"Bodyguard, ay?" The older man raised an eyebrow to Keth who gave a brief nod. Darin gave a loud bird call and a boy appeared. "Run ahead to the camp and tell them Milord's back."

The boy nodded and disappeared again.

"Darin."

"Yes, Milord?"

"There were Hunters out."

"Any of them get away, Milord?"

"No."

"I'll make sure to pass it on to the others to increase their vigilance." The older man nodded to Pierce, then vanished.

"How does he do that?"

Keth gave a laugh. "I don't know how any of the Foresters do it either. I know it's not sight-bending though."

"Actually, it is," Hawk said in a low voice. "Just a different version than you're used to. Instead of causing the sight to blur, it fools the mind into not seeing at all."

"How do you know that?" Keth looked at Hawk.

"Because I see differently."

Keth stared at him for a moment, then kneed his mount to start it walking.

"You can tell when someone is using mind-power?" It was Beka who asked the question they were all thinking.

"I have all my natural abilities in this body."

"There are many tales of Dragconic deeds, but they're just that, tales, to most of us." Beka told him. "So much is unknown to us."

"What has happened to the world that such is only tales?"

"I thought you had access to some of his memories," Pierce commented. "There should be such knowledge in them."

"Body memory." Hawk paused, then said, "I remember the Plague and starting my sleep, but nothing really after that."

"What about when you were in my mind?"

"Just flashes," Hawk said, as if to reassure her, which is what she needed, wanted. "I only have an empathic link unless I touch your mind on purpose."

Beka had tensed in anticipation of his answer and now she relaxed at his words. The thought of someone continually lodged in her mind scared her.

Warchild halted and Keth pulled up his mount just in time to miss the sentry that suddenly appeared. "Milord."

"Elly."

The leather-clad young woman gave a laugh. "Almost got ya. If it wasn't for the Steed, I would have."

"True enough. I'll pay more attention to my

surroundings."

"Good." With a toss of her head, she whipped her long braid back over her shoulder and gave the others a once over, lingering over Hawk. "I heard there was a bit of trouble."

"It was taken care of," Keth assured her. "I'll give a meeting later."

"I'm looking forward to it." Elly gave him a brief smile, her eyes flickering back to Hawk. "Who's our new ones?"

"Nice try, Elly." Keth shook his head at her. "His name's Hawk and he bites."

"Really?" Elly batted her eyes at Hawk who meet her eyes. She suddenly swallowed and stepped back. "I'll see ya later, Milord."

Keth watched her disappear with a faint smile, then looked at Hawk. "I can see you'll be popular."

"I'm not here to be popular."

"Elly's harmless, but there's a lot of people in camp that will try and test you, no matter what I say."

"As long as they leave Beka alone, I'll leave them alone," Hawk told him.

"All I can ask," Keth said, starting his mount forward again. "We should be at the camp soon."

"Home sweet home," Pierce said as Warchild followed Keth's mount eagerly.

Keth kept them at a fast walk, apparently just as eager to get to the camp before darkness fell.

The mounts finally halted at the entrance of a canyon and the camp was spread out before them. A stream backed the camp as well as a group of trees that covered part of the valley that seemed to surround the camp.

"Wow. It's like a town."

"It's listed as a town actually," Pierce told her. "A mining town to be exact."

"To explain all the movement, right?"

"And all the holes in the walls," Keth answered her this time. "Traders even come by every now and then."

An old man came up to them as they entered the town and grabbed the reins of Keth's mount. "Milord."

"Lor."

"The others are gathering at Grey's tavern."

"Thank you, Lor." Keth dismounted and gestured for Pierce and Beka to do so as well. "Will you take Dana and Warchild to my stables?"

"Of course, Milord."

"How are we going to handle this?" Pierce asked as they started walking.

"By saying as little as possible," Keth replied. "After all, what isn't said, can't be thrown back at us later."

"True enough."

Few people were about, but those that were gave Keth and Pierce nods or a little wave as they passed along the street. Some of the buildings housed workshops, others businesses of all types, even a bakery. Keth lead them down a side street and the buildings thinned out, becoming residential. Finally they were in front of a tavern and Keth paused.

"Are you ready to meet my sub-leaders?"

"Not like we got much choice now, ay?" Beka replied while Hawk just shrugged.

Pierce opened the door silently, and Keth moved forward into the tavern's front room.

# CHAPTER V

"Good evening, gentlemen and lady," Keth said to those awaiting them. "It's good to see you all."

Beka stepped in and stayed behind Keth and Pierce, her eyes taking in the three men and one woman that were seated at a table by the fireplace. One of the men was mousy haired, but the other two were blond as was the woman who wore her hair in a braid like Elly's. All were gray-eyed and were older than Keth, though younger than Pierce.

The other twelve tables were empty as was the bar area though a man stood in a door near the bar that probably led to the kitchen area. A set of stairs led upward from near the large fireplace which no doubt led to the tavern's rented rooms or even the owner's own rooms.

"Before we start, let me introduce you to my niece Beka Lane." Keth paused as he stepped aside, revealing Beka to the others. "Beka, this is the 'town Council'. Your other Uncle Wills--he's the Representative for the miners. Saven Wells for the farmers, Raum Dans for the merchants." He gestured to the men. "And Jax Mays for the Tavern owners."

"Mercy's?" the mousy-haired Wills asked with a raised eyebrow.

"Yes," Keth nodded. "And this is Dylan Hawk, bodyguard."

"Welcome to Yagos," the two blonde men said in harmony.

"They do that often," the woman, Jax, said with a smile. "If we didn't know any better we'd think they were twins instead of cousins."

"Okay, now that we've all been introduced, let's get to it." Wills became serious. "What happened at the meet?"

"Kerr Ivery set us up." Keth paused. "Ken, can we have a couple of mugs here?"

The man in the doorway nodded and disappeared into the room behind him.

"What happened?" Wills repeated.

"He showed up early with an attitude and we were attacked."

"So everything he told us was lies?" Raum asked.

"Right now I wouldn't believe him if he told me the sun was going to come up tomorrow," Keth said. "He probably used whatever he needed to get us where he wanted us."

"We've been hearing that he kidnapped a Messenger," Jax told Keth. "Do you think that's true?"

Pierce and Beka both jerked their heads up to stare at her.

"That's probably true. Calli was attacked at a meet," Keth said, carefully not looking at Pierce. "What exactly is the rumor?"

Jax gave Pierce a look, then turned her attention to Keth. "A group of riders stopped at Caren's tavern yesterday and they were talking about a messenger that their lord was questioning. Caren didn't get any names but the men were wearing Ivery's livery. Before that Caren had talked to a runner and he said that Kerr Ivery had taken a Messenger to his manor. We didn't know that it could be Calli or we would have inquired further."

"Is the runner still here?" Pierce asked.

"No, he left last night."

"Keth…"

"I know, Pierce. We'll see what we can do."

The man from the doorway returned with a tray of mugs and a pitcher. He handed out the mugs, then refilled the mugs of the people at the table before moving back to the kitchen doorway.

"You think Kerr Ivery is taking the quest for the Heart seriously?" Wills leaned back and took a sip. "Or did he just take her to get our location?"

"And did she have it when he took her?" Jax added.

"I don't think Kerr Ivery is taking it seriously, but the King of Rennon is." Keth sipped from his own mug. "His soldiers in the Borderlands are moving in the mountains."

"Strife and madness!" Wills exclaimed.

"You sure the alert's for the Heart?" Jax asked with a look at Beka and Hawk. "Mayhap they're for something else."

"What do you mean, Jax?" Keth asked calmly.

"How do we know these two are who you say they are?"

Pierce growled and took a step forward, but Keth held out a hand to stop him. "You saying I would be fooled by spies?"

Beka watched the expressive faces of Raum and Saven for a moment, then met the eyes of Jax squarely. It was a legitimate question. They didn't know her, and all this had happened when she had shown up. Hawk had shifted closer to her, and she could  feel his concern for her. But neither of them spoke, allowing Keth to meet the challenge.

"Best way to infiltrate the resistance," Jax said, her voice carefully neutral. "And you are vulnerable right now."

"Kit has been dead for over a year now, Jax. If they had wanted to go that route they would have done it sooner." Keth sighed. "And I thought better of you."

"Kit?" Beka asked in the sudden silence.

"My late wife." Keth took a large gulp from his mug. "Beka is Mercy's child, Jax, of that I am sure."

"She could still be a spy," Jax said stubbornly. "Or the hulking male could be."

"What do you want from me, Jax," Keth asked

her.

"You," Hawk said. "She's got feelings for you."

Keth blinked, then looked at the blush on Jax's cheeks.

"Well, that explains a lot," Pierce said.

Raum and Saven relaxed in their chairs, while Wills took a sip from his mug. "Certainly does."

"You had no right…" Jax began.

"He had every right if your feelings were disrupting your common sense," Keth interrupted. "She's my niece for Strife's sake, not anything else."

"We still don't know anything about them," Jax insisted.

"I just spent the last few days with her," Pierce said. "And she's not shy about talking."

"Enough," Wills said to Jax. "Bruised feelings aside you have nothing to base this suspicion on."

"There is a connection between the two of them, Wills," Saven said softly. "I can feel it, but it doesn't seem—evil."

"He's not human," Jax blurted out. "Can't you feel that!"

"You really should leave well enough alone, woman," Hawk said, his eyes flashing an emerald green.

"How…" Beka laid a hand on his arm.

"She's an empath, a strong receptive empath with mid-level active empathy."

"And constantly scanning you," Keth said.

"Yes."

"Keth?"

Keth met his brother's eyes briefly before

looking at Jax. "You will stop that now."

Jax raised her chin, then suddenly clutched her head with a moan. "Stop!"

"When you do," Hawk replied.

"Keth!"

"It's all right, Wills," Keth told him. "He won't kill her."

"So much for not telling," Pierce commented.

"As long as most of your people don't know who I am," Hawk told him. "I still will hold you to your promise."

"We have other Empaths, some stronger than Jax."

"But they won't be constantly scanning," Keth said. "I think that's what caught him out."

"Correct. My affect is mainly flat since I'm not really here." Hawk paused as Jax sagged in her chair. "She's withdrawn into herself."

"Keth." Wills' voice made the name something between a question and a statement of intent.

"Hawk?"

Hawk didn't answer; he was staring at Raum and Saven. Both were frozen.

"Hawk?" Keth repeated.

"I'm not hurting them." Hawk turned his attention to Wills. "Don't fight me, Wills Shallan."

"What are you doing, Hawk?" Keth looked at Hawk.

"They will not be able to talk about what they have learned about me."

"Don't..." Jax whimpered when Hawk looked at her.

"I could just burn out your brain," Hawk told

her. "Your choice."

"Hawk…" Keth began.

"Don't forget the innkeeper," Beka said with a glance at the man in the doorway.

"Beka…"

"What?" Beka looked at Keth. "You'd rather he kill them?"

Hawk suddenly paled and his hand snaked out to grip Beka's arm. He seemed to sag for a moment, then straightened, almost as if he was drawing strength from her.

Beka herself felt Hawk as if he was sitting in her mind. Which she guessed he was.

"So you're not invulnerable," Pierce commented.

"No mortal creature is," Hawk replied, looking at both Pierce and Keth. "I am limited to the energy contained within the body I wear, the physical condition of said body, and the distance from my true self."

"What did you do to us?" Raum asked as he rubbed his temples. Saven was still holding his head and Jax was cowering in her chair. The innkeeper was leaning against the door frame and holding his head as well. Wills was the only one who seemed not to be affected by what Hawk did.

"I just made it so you can't talk to anyone about me."

"Why didn't you do that to me and Pierce?"

"Do I need to?" Hawk met Keth's eyes.

"That doesn't answer my question," Keth told him, holding his eyes steady.

"Don't be dense, Keth," Wills said, looking at Keth. "You're not stupid."

"Neither are you," Hawk looked at Wills. "You knew who I was the minute you saw me."

"Before Jax..?" Pierce asked.

"Yes." Hawk pulled Beka to him and held her close, his eyes going to Jax. He buried his nose in Beka's hair and took a deep breath.

Jax gave a shudder and Beka felt Hawk smile. He was radiating protectiveness with a bit of smugness.

"What are you doing, Hawk?"

"Setting boundaries." Hawk raised his head, his eyes sliding sideways to Keth. "For everyone."

"As I've stated, she's my niece, nothing else."

"I just want to make sure we're all on the same page," Hawk said. "I will not allow her or myself to be used."

"And she's tired of being talked about as if she isn't here," Beka said, elbowing Hawk in the ribs. She wasn't going to let him get away with that.

"I don't think that will be a problem," Pierce told Hawk with a laugh.

"Perhaps not," Hawk said, rubbing his side.

"We really need to talk about what we're going to do with you two," Keth said. "There's no room in my home for you."

"Nor in mine or Jens'," Wills said. "And the women are pregnant and don't need extra in their homes anyway."

"The old livery," the innkeeper said. "There are quarters above the stables."

"A very good idea, Ken." Keth paused. "And it can be fixed up to working order quite readily."

"I was helping Da to run the stables at the inn."

Her own stables. Da would be proud. If she made a good go of them, that is.

"Excellent…"

"We can work out the details tomorrow." Wills waved a hand. "I think we all need time right now."

Saven and Raum grunted their agreement as they were still holding their heads.

"They can stay the night here." The innkeeper paused, glancing at Jax. "But the sooner they're set up, the better all around."

"Agreed." Keth gave a nod. "Beka, Hawk?"

"As long as we have connecting rooms," Hawk said.

Beka nodded.

"I'll send up a meal as well," the innkeeper said. "First two rooms on the right."

"Jax, Raum call a general meeting for tonight." Keth said as Beka and Hawk stood. "I'll tell them about the meet and that I brought back my niece."

"I don't have to be there?" Beka asked him

"Only if you want."

"No." Beka shook her head. "I'll see you in the morning."

Both she and Hawk went up the stairs as Keth and Pierce wished them goodnight.

# CHAPTER VI

Beka stared at the ceiling in the dim morning light as sleep slowly loosened its grip on her.

The others had left after she, with Hawk in tow, had headed upstairs. Along with the promised meal, the innkeeper had sent up her saddle bag and some water for washing. Beka had been more than grateful for that. Traveling with two men hadn't given her many opportunities for more than the briefest of washes.

She and Hawk had also had a brief talk.

Dragons were drawn to their bonded. However, the way in which they were drawn was different for each Dragon as well as the strength of the bond. The bond was platonic but whether it was merely mental or soulmate or both depended upon the human's soul.

A knock on the half-open connecting door drew her attention and Hawk was standing there. He was wearing a pair of farmer's overalls, and over his arm he was carrying a pair of workman's coveralls. "The innkeeper sent you these. He said you'll need them too if you plan to clean the stables completely."

"If the livery hasn't been kept up then he's right," Beka said with a stretch. "Did he say anything about meeting with the others again?"

"Just that Keth will meet us downstairs for breakfast in a few minutes."

"Then go on down and I'll be there in a minute."

Hawk laid the coveralls on the chair by the bed and silently left.

Beka threw off the covers and got out of bed. She had slept in only her tunic, too tired to dig out her dirty nightclothes from the saddle bag. All her clothes needed washing. Once the livery was set to rights, laundry was next. That decided, she slipped on a pair of pants before pulling on the over-sized coveralls.

Grabbing her saddlebag, she headed downstairs. Keth and Hawk were sitting at a table near the fireplace with plates in front of them. Beka slid into a seat next to Hawk, hanging her saddlebag on the back of the chair.

"Morning, Beka."

"Morning, Uncle."

The innkeeper came in with another plate and set it before her. He took her saddlebag off the back of the chair and handed it to the woman that came in with him. "These will get washed while you all work on the livery."

"Thank you."

With a laugh the innkeeper and the woman head back into the kitchen.

"My daughter Theo will meet us at the livery. She and the boys, Tad and Jak, Merry's sons, are already there. I told them to do the mattresses since they can just throw them out the loft door."

"Is anyone else going to be there?"

"Just Wills and Jens, I think." Keth gave a wry smile. "I think the others will be leaving you pretty much alone."

Hawk just shrugged at the look both Beka and Keth gave him.

"The livery's necessity should still be in good shape since the miners use the shower there sometimes. I'll have Jens check it out when we get there."

"What about the quarters in the loft?" Beka cleaned her plate with her last bite of toast, then drained her mug. "Are they divided into rooms or just partitioned?"

"Rooms. Three to be exact." Keth pushed his own plate away. "One for the stable boys sleeping area, one for the master with a fireplace, and another with a small kitchen."

"The one for the master is partitioned?"

"Yes."

"Well the work ain't going to do itself," Beka said as she slid her chair back.

Hawk pushed away from the table and stood.

"Unfortunately not," Keth sigh as he too stood. "The livery ain't been touched in over two years since the last owner died. While the hay was removed, everything else was left as it was."

"So no one has a claim on it?" Beka asked as she and Hawk headed toward the door with Keth behind them.

"Jon didn't have any kin." Keth followed her into the street and moved to walk beside her. "They all died off during the last bout of Summer Fever."

"Like Ma and Sali," Beka said.

"There's been speculation about whether Summer Fever is natural or not. It hits those of Borderland blood the hardest, though it does strike Eldanian pretty hard as well."

"I was pretty sick," Beka said thoughtfully. "Could it be a version of what the Old King of Rennon had let loose during the Year of Death?"

"That's a thought," Keth said just as thoughtfully. "Brings up all kinds of thoughts actually."

"The current King could be using it to 'soften up' the Eldanians." Hawk paused. "If he was thinking of taking over at least part of Eldan. It is sound and proven strategy."

Keth rubbed his face with a sigh. "So it is."

They stopped in front of a large wooden building with two men leaning against it. One of the men was Wills, the other man was mousy haired but finer boned than either Wills or Keth. He straightened and gave a half-bow to Beka.

"I'm your uncle Jens. We'll have to talk sometimes about Mercy, when we all have more time to relax."

"We'll have to do that." Beka gave both men a nod.

"Theo and the boys tossed them out and we moved them over there out of the way." Wills gestured to the mattresses lying in the road and grass to their right. "I told Theo to stay upstairs and for the boys to come on down."

"Good. I don't think we'll need to work on the blacksmithing area." Keth gave a gesture to the lean-to area attached to the livery.

"At least not right now," Hawk said. "I can work on it later."

Keth gave Hawk's muscular frame a look but did not comment.

"Right," Wills said. "Then let's get to it."

As they turned to enter the building, two teenaged mousy haired boys came out. The oldest was probably about fourteen or fifteen and the other boy was about two years younger. They too were dressed in coveralls.

"Tad, you and Jak, go back to the necessity with Jens. I know the miners use the shower part sometimes, but the rest of it probably needs seeing to."

"I'd rather clean the stables," the younger boy said.

"I know, Jak. But you know you have to sometimes do things you don't want to do." Keth told the boy. "If you get it done before lunch, then after you can help us with the stables."

"Okay." The boy, Jak, seemed to brighten.

The other boy, Tad, just rolled his eyes and

dragged his brother around the side of the building. Jens sighed and followed.

"I gather Jak's an aspiring stableman?"

"Yep," Keth laughed. "Tad's wanting to work metal, but our only blacksmith already has three apprentices."

"Perhaps we can do something about both," Hawk said with a glance at Beka.

"Perhaps," she agreed.

The other two men exchanged glances but didn't say anything.

"Shall we get started?"

All four entered the livery which was lit by several lanterns and the two open windows. A third window looked into the blacksmithing lean-to and brought in only a little light. Dirt covered everything and towards the back was a staircase and a door. Near the front was a ladder leading to a small hayloft where a tackle hung. The stables themselves looked to be in good condition which relieved Beka greatly.

"It will take a full wagon for the hay loft." Beka moved to the stairs with the others following. "I'd rather get the living quarters done before lunch then tackle the stables this afternoon."

"I told Theo and the boys to bring cleaning supplies when they came so everything should be upstairs," Keth told her as they hurried up the stairs. "I checked the pump in the kitchen yesterday."

"Good."

They paused on the landing and Beka noticed there were four doors instead of three. One of the doors was open and she heard movement inside.

"Theo?" Keth called out to his daughter.

"I'm in the kitchen," came a soft voice.

The four of them went through the open door into a large room with a cook stove, sink and cabinets on one side and a pair of couches on the other. A mousy teenager in coveralls was cleaning the sink. She appeared to be all arms and legs and thin as a rail.

"What did you do to make the boys leave?" Keth asked.

The girl straightened and turned towards them. "Nothing."

"Why don't I believe you?" Keth shook his head. "This is your cousin Beka that I told you about and her bodyguard, Hawk."

"Hi." Theo gave a little wave.

"Hello," Beka said as Hawk gave a nod.

"Should we divide the other rooms up or work together in one room?" Keth picked up a bucket and a broom with a dustpan from beside the door. "Each room has a dust bin."

"Divide and conquer." Beka grabbed the other bucket and shoved it into Hawk's hands before she took the broom and dustpan. "One dusts and sweeps while the other starts the walls. I can see someone started to work on these walls."

"The boys no doubt." Keth looked at Theo. "You going to be okay in here by yourself?"

The girl rolled her eyes and went back to cleaning the sink.

"I think that was a yes." Beka smiled.

Keth shook his head and lead the way back onto the landing. "The stableboys' quarters has two bunk beds and a heating stove. I don't think it needs more than sweeping and the stove looked at."

"There's four doors."

"One leads into the loft." Keth gestured to the door on the left.

Beka nodded acknowledgment. "Which do you want?"

"We'll take the bunk room." Wills spoke up.

"Right." Beka opened a door and found she had chosen right as it opened into a room that was divided in two. The larger section had a double bed while the other had two twin beds. Each section had a wardrobe and a small chest. A heating stove rested in the section with the double bed.

She sent Hawk for some water while she stepped farther into the room. He returned moments later, and she set him to washing the walls. She got to work on the floors.

They had worked silently at this for a few hours when a loud knock made them stop and look toward the door. A heavily pregnant woman was standing on the landing with a tray carrying a pitcher and some mugs.

"I think a break is in order." The woman set the tray on a small table that had been set nearby. "And I thought you all could use a drink."

"Zana." Wills appeared from the other room and moved to carefully hug the woman.

Keth moved to the tray and picked up a mug. "Thanks, Zana."

The blonde woman blushed faintly as Wills kept his arms around her middle, just above her extended stomach. "Beka, this is my wife, Zana."

"Pleased to meet you,Zana." Beka said, grabbing one of the mugs. "Especially with this."

"Well, I also came to get Theo. She said she would be helping me."

"I'm ready." Theo came out of the kitchen. "The sink and table's done. I did the wall around the sink and started on the one behind the stove."

"Thank you." Beka smiled at the girl.

Theo gave a shy smile.

"I came to get you, young lady," Zana said. "I was expecting you some time ago."

"I got carried away." The girl ducked her head. "I'm sorry."

"That's okay," Beka said as the girl stepped forward. "Less work for me. Thanks for your help."

"You're welcome."

"Well, come along, girl," Zana said, patting Wills hands again. "We got things to do."

"Right." Wills reluctantly let Zana go. "I'll bring the mugs back at lunch."

"Good. See you later, dear."

The woman went down the stairs with the girl by her side while the others drained their mugs and set them back on the tray.

"Lunch is two hours away. Think we'll have the rest of this done by then."

"Within the hour, actually," Beka told Wills. "The master bedroom's done. The stove's the only thing left."

"I already had it looked at," Keth told her.

"Good." She paused as she thought over her next words. "Would you mind doing the stables while I shop this afternoon? I just realized we have nothing we need.”

“This may seem indelicate, but do you have any coin?”

“This one had a full purse.” Hawk tapped his chest. “I also have my hoard. There is more than enough ‘coin’ for her when she needs it.”

“Just checking.” Keth put his hands up in surrender. “Well, let’s get to it. The sooner it’s done the sooner we eat.”

“Should we check on the boys before we start again?” Wills asked.

Keth gave him a sideways glance. “Go ahead, Wills.”

All of them laughed as Wills nearly ran down the stairs. While he ‘checked on’ the boys, the others started on the rest of the kitchen. True to Beka’s words the work was done in less than an hour.

Jens, Wills and the boys joined them a few minutes later on the landing.

“We went ahead and swept the stables,” Jens said. “All that needs done is putting the hay in the loft when the farmer comes after lunch.”

“I wondered what was taking you so long.” Keth shook his head. “Well and good. You and Wills can do that. I have a meeting after lunch and Beka needs to do some shopping.”

“So back here in two hours?” Wills asked Jens.

“Yes.” Jens nodded. “I’ll help with the mugs.”

Wills picked up the tray and Jens grabbed the table, and both men went down the stairs with the boys.

“You need any help with the shopping?”

“I’ll use Hawk as a mule.”

"Okay." Keth headed down the stairs with them on his heels. Once in the livery, they moved to the front doors and turned towards Grey's Tavern. "Ken will feed us though he usually ain't open till after noon."

"I noticed there were no others at breakfast."

"He opens for the after noon crowd and mostly for the evening crowd. Last night was an exception. He had some problems, but they're fixed so he'll be open tonight."

"So it'll be best if we're in the livery tonight then."

"All around. Jax…"

"She wouldn't remember much of last night," Hawk interrupted. "Neither will the innkeeper. The two men will remember more, but Wills will be the only one who remembers the whole thing."

"So she won't remember you revealing her…"

"No." Hawk shook his head. "But you need to do something about it or it will get worse."

"I just can't believe it."

"Her feelings run deep for you. You need to decide what you want and soon."

"Perhaps you should talk with Theo as well," Beka said. "See what she wants as well."

"Perhaps I should."

They paused at the door to remove the coveralls before entering the dim tavern and finding a seat. The innkeeper came out with a tray of mugs and bowls almost immediately. "I thought it was about time for you to show up."

"We only have the loft to do."

"Good. Good." The innkeeper rubbed his hands

together. "My wife is finished washing your clothes, Miss Beka, but she found some tears. She just can't let that go."

"Tell her I appreciate that."

The innkeeper waved his hand. "It's nothing."

Keth raised his eyebrow but let the comment pass for now as he started to eat.

"Is there a good tanner in town?" Hawk asked the innkeeper before he could leave.

"Oh, two, sir. Each have different specialties. One is best at boots and clothing, while the other for tack."

"Clothing."

"That would be Bell. Jak Bell."

"Thank you."

The innkeeper left and Keth looked at Hawk. "You said something about your hoard."

Hawk closed his one hand into a fist and when he opened it a small gem sat on his palm. "Dragons can teleport small objects like a gem or a handful of coins."

"So the tales of Dragons hoarding gold and gems is true?"

"Humans gave such things to keep us from burning down their villages and to pay for works we did for them." Hawk handed the gem to Beka. "We also found some when we carved out our caves."

They ate silently for awhile, then pushed aside their bowls. The innkeeper came out with a pitcher, then took the bowls back to the kitchen. Mugs were refilled, then Keth looked at Hawk.

"What did you mean about fixing up the smithy later?"

"While this one was a mercenary, he was also a Farrier."

"Will that skill transfer?"

"The weapons training did as you saw," Hawk replied. "I will test it out first, of course."

"Unlike the weapons skill?" Beka said, dryly.

Hawk just shrugged.

"Where are your weapons?"

"The innkeeper sent them to the blacksmith." Hawk pulled out a knife. "They will be delivered later to the livery."

"Just don't kill anyone, all right?" Keth took a sip from his mug. "No matter how obnoxious they are."

"Rude, I can handle," Hawk told him. "Vicious I will not."

"Fair enough, I guess."

"You should worry more about what *I* will do to them. I don't like rude people."

Keth smiled, then frowned as Beka pulled out a small knife.

"Da, taught me to protect myself. A female working in a stable is considered fair game, you know, just like a farmer's daughter."

"I wandered why you weren't wed by now."

"Da kept most of the riff raff away and others learned to be wary of me after a while. Though the innkeeper's son wouldn't keep away for long." She still didn't know why, since she had tried it a few times with a few of her father's stable boys and hadn't found it all that pleasurable.

Keth frowned, then glanced at a grim Hawk. "Here that shouldn't be a problem."

"Good." She slipped her knife away. "We're going to be needing bedding too, I just realized."

"Not a problem. Nettie Ree and her sister are our main weavers and they should be starting on some bedding already. Ken will lend you some for awhile until Nettie's done with a least a set for you."

"As in Ben Ree, Jak and Tad's father, right?"

Yes. He's a sheep farmer and the boys mostly stay with Nettie since it's an easier commute to school."

"I'm not used to this. Da and my brothers were all I had, now I got all these relatives."

"You'll get used to it."

"I hope so."

The innkeeper came back in and retrieved the mugs before hurrying back to the kitchen. Keth stretched then pushed away from the table. "There is only one true clothing shop. It's next to the grocers on the main street. The tanners are on a side street."

Hawk frowned, but Beka shrugged. "Then we'll split up and meet back at the livery."

The dragon's frown deepened.

"You can't be with me all the time, Hawk. "

"Yes, I can."

"Hawk." She added a bit of warning in her tone. After all she was perfectly able to take care of herself. She wasn't a child.

"All right." Hawk stood up and moved to the door. "Nothing better happen."

"What's going to happen here?"

# CHAPTER VII

The faint sickly sweet taste of Coren was the first thing she became aware of; the ropes binding her were the second. She was in a box of some kind, in something moving; a wagon no doubt by the roughness of the movement. Coren explained the blankness in her memory of how she got here; once deeply inhaled or drank, one became unconscious for varied periods of time, hence its use during surgery.

She remembered visiting the clothing store--and the conversation with Hawk beforehand. He'd never let her out of his sight now. The thought was actually comforting instead of stifling as it had been earlier today.

A rumble of voices came from above and the

movement around her abruptly stopped. There were three loud clicks and she was suddenly blinded by sunlight. Hands rolled her and before she could even think about struggling, she was slung over a shoulder. However, she didn't attempt to fight, but instead lifted her head enough to look around.

Looking sideways she saw what looked like a caravan camp. Tents formed a half circle around a low-burning fire while to the left was a string of staked animals. She glanced at the men moving around her while the one carrying her headed towards the larger of the tents. They were all dressed in the loose clothing of caravan runners but there were bulges in interesting places and their movements were more wary than relaxed as they took the wagon away. That they were camped and not on the road traveling made this camp suspicious and should make it easier for it to be found.

The man carrying her ducked into the tent, then she felt the ropes around her legs give way. She was set unceremoniously on her feet and the man removed her gag before stepping away from her.

"Welcome, young Messenger."

"You."

The man she had last seen in the company of Kerr Ivery chuckled.

"What are you doing here?"

"Hunting you," he explained with a small smile.

"Who the strife are you?"

"Zebada is good enough for now."

"Zebada was the name of an old Rennon traitor and murderer."

"You're very well educated, young Messenger."

"My name is Beka Lane," she told him with a glare. "What do you want with me, spy?"

"Direct and to the point. Such a refreshing change."

"What. Do. You. Want?" she asked him again.

"Why the Dragon's Heart, of course." He paused as she started laughing. "I'm so glad I amuse you."

Beka made an effort to control her laughter, then looked at Zebada. "Did you find it on my person?"

"Oh, I don't think you have it now." Zebada waved his hand. "But you know where it is."

"It's beyond any man's reach." She was oddly not afraid of him nor of her situation. He disgusted her but she didn't fear him.

"For your sake, you'd best be wrong."

"Or what? You'll kill me?" Again that thought did not bring fear.

"And that lady Messenger I took from Kerr Ivery."

"Mistress Penn?" Anxiety twisted her stomach then as she thought of her mistress.

"Yes."

"Wait a minute, I thought you worked for Kerr Ivery."

"So did he, poor fellow. He developed a severe case of steel poisoning not long after that travesty in the forest."

"Killing us isn't going to get you the Dragon's Heart." She paused, meeting his dark Rennon eyes. While she was feeling anxiety for Calli there was still no true fear for herself. "I told you it's beyond any man's reach."

"Perhaps some time with your former mistress

will change your mind." Zebada gestured to the guard. "Take her to where the other prisoner is."

The guard grabbed Beka's still bound arms and dragged her toward the opening.

"Oh, and if you're waiting for rescue, don't. We're a plague caravan. No one will come here."

Beka didn't resist the guard when he dragged her thru the opening as she digested that news. True most would stay away from any caravan flying the plague flag, but her uncle would know that it was still suspicious. And Hawk would definitely know that she was here. *He* would not be afraid of any "plague".

She relaxed into a roll when the guard shoved her into a smaller tent, ending up in a pile of hay. Hands helped her sit up and she was suddenly face to face with her mistress. "Mistress…"

"Can't say I'm glad to see you, girl," came the soft voice. "But I am glad you're alive."

Her clothes were ripped and bruises adorned her exposed skin, but she seemed the same Calli Penn that Beka had ridden with just a short time ago.

"Are you okay, Mistress?"

"I think you can call me Calli, girl."

"Then I'm Beka," Beka replied with a bit of spirit.

Calli gave a brief chuckle. "Beka it is then. I should be asking if *you're* alright. These heavy-handed louts."

"I'm fine. I was only drugged. Zebada hasn't tried anything with me yet."

"Yet, being the operative word. A sadist that one."

"I told him that the Heart was beyond any man's reach but I can tell he didn't believe me so I expect to be seeing him later."

"Any man's reach," Calli recited slowly, her eyes on Beka. "No, a man like Zabada wouldn't believe that."

"He will soon enough," Beka said with a small smile.

"Yeah, about the time a fireball hits him," Calli said with a smile of her own.

"Perhaps that can be arranged." Good. She understood.

"I hope so."

"Now what happened at the inn after I left?" Beka asked, changing the topic in case the guard was listening. "I saw liveried men."

"Kerr Ivery's guard happened. I had just finished with the ones he'd sent to delay me when the others showed up. I kept them busy since I knew I had to buy you time."

"There were rumors that Kerr Ivery had a Messenger."

"Not for long." Calli gave a little chuckle. "Zebada doesn't suffer fools it seems."

"He seemed a good little minion at the stables."

"Well, he's a skilled interrogator." Calli paused as she rubbed her left shoulder. "I'm glad I didn't have anything to tell that he didn't already know."

Beka raised an eyebrow but was reassured by Calli's wink. "I wonder whose minion he really is."

"If he's a minion," Calli said thoughtfully.

"Very perceptive of you, Messenger Penn," Zebada said as he entered, the guard behind him. "I had hoped you would have spent this time persuading your apprentice to make it easier on herself and just tell me what I want to know."

"Like you would believe anything I'd tell you that way," Beka said.

"True enough," Zebada gave a little smile. "Now let's get down to it, shall we…"

The guard stepped forward and unexpectedly hit Zebada on the back of his head. Zebada dropped like a stone and the guard looked at Beka. "I told you I should have stayed with you."

Beka met the green eyes of the guard. "Hawk."

Stepping over Zebada, the guard moved to Beka's side and cut her bonds. "We don't have much time."

"We need to take him with us," Calli said with a gesture toward Zebada.

"Why?"

"Because of who he is." Calli paused as Hawk moved to tie Zebada's hands. "Or at least who I suspect he is."

"All right…Did you tell Keth what happened, Hawk?"

"What I knew. We're not far behind, though this camp is a ways from Yagos."

"So we're on our own then for now?" Beka frowned.

"Yes."

"Great."

Hawk threw Zebada over his shoulder and moved to the opening. "I'm going to try to fool them into not seeing us, but with controlling this body it might not be complete."

"Shields?"

"Not anymore."

"Ah." Beka realized what that meant. "Mistress, please stay close."

"Don't worry about that."

Beka hooked her hand into Hawk's guard belt while Calli grabbed a handful of Beka's tunic. "We're ready."

Hawk ducked out the opening at her words, and the world around them seemed to suddenly shimmer as a sight-bending field activated around them. Beka could almost feel the effort Hawk was using to keep the field extended around them. They made it to where the horses were corralled, and Hawk stopped. The field faded away as they each grabbed a haltered horse. Zebada was slung over one, then Hawk slipped onto that horse's back as Calli and Beka swung onto their horses. A yell came from their left and they kicked their horses into a gallop, dodging to the right, edging out of the mass of horseflesh.

Beka kept her horse at the heels of the one that Hawk rode, Calli following her. She knew if they were caught this time it wouldn't be easy on them.

Arrows started flying around them, but their evasive course had so far kept any of them from getting hit. The horse ahead of her faltered for a second, then continued, but an arrow had struck the shoulder of the body Hawk was using. Even as she watched, another skimmed the horse's flank, causing it to falter again. An arrow struck Hawk's temporary body in the middle of his back, causing him to fall from the saddle.

Beka moved her own horse beside the guard's and pulled them both to a stop. She slid over onto the other horse and held her small blade against Zebada as Calli reined in beside her.

The body lay unmoving on the ground a few feet away as the camp's guards stopped their own mounts.

"I'm not going back." Beka told them, her knife steady.

"You have no choice," one of the guards told her. "Now let that little sticker drop and come along."

"Why don't you all just go back and leave us be?"

The guards all laughed.

"Do as she says or you'll be minus a leader," Calli told them.

"You ain't going to hurt him," the guard who had spoke before said. "So just come along or we'll have to get rough."

"I'm not going back."

"And you ain't going anywhere else!"

Beka stared at the guards for a long moment, then smiled as a tendril touched her mind. Anger and rage was being projected but there was also a fierce protectiveness present.

A shadow swept over the group and everyone but Beka looked up. The large form made another pass over them, then landed near the group, causing the horses to go wild.

The dragon seemed to be a mixture of feline and reptile. A broad large-eyed head, oddly reminiscent of a cat's, rose upon a long and flexible neck. The wings, vast seeming as they were when in flight, were neatly folded along the muscular back while a thick flexible tail was curled around the cruel-looking talons of the forefeet and hid the rear talons of one rear claw.

Once everyone had their steeds under control, Beka glanced over, briefly meeting one of the dragon's jewel-toned eyes and gave a small nod. "We're going to go now."

One of the guards shifted and the dragon rumbled.

"I'd advise you to stay very still," Beka told them as she and Calli carefully backed their horses further from the dragon before turning them. As soon as the horses were turned they were kicked into a gallop.

"So that was Panas," Calli said in a wondering tone as the horses slowed to a trot.

"Do you know where we are?" Beka was more worried about the here and now, than Hawk's real name. All they could do right now was head the way Hawk had been taking them and hope it was the right direction.

"Not really. We have to still be near the Borderlands though." Calli made a gesture to the mountainous horizon on their left. "Your guard friend said we were 'a ways' from Yagos, but that doesn't tell us much."

"Hawk said they weren't far behind us."

"So hopefully we'll run into them if we keep going." Calli glanced behind them. "Before Zebada's men get up the nerve to try something again."

"I doubt they'll try to get around a dragon." She knew he was still keeping the guards occupied.

"How'd it happen?"

Beka glanced sideways at her, not even pretending to not understand. "An arrow through the back. I really don't remember, but you can ask Keth since he was there."

Calli glanced behind them again. "What's it like?"

"I don't feel any different probably because he keeps out of my mind for the most part. I think he's afraid he'll scare me."

"I didn't think they felt fear like we do," Calli told her. "What is written about them…"

"They feel a lot of things, I think. More so than humans, I believe." At least Hawk did. Even without him actively in her mind she still felt his emotions.

Before Calli could say anything, Beka felt movement from Zebada and suddenly pulled her horse to a stop.

Calli slowed her own horse, then joined Beka. "Waking is he?"

"He's moving anyway. Are you awake, Spy?"

"My men will catch up to you soon."

"They already did, spy, but as you see they didn't hold us."

"They wouldn't have let you go."

"Well, they didn't have much choice." Calli gave a grim laugh.

Zebada shifted, then froze as he felt Beka's small knife at his throat.

"Calli seems to think you're worth something

alive, but personally I'd just as soon kill you and leave you here. You behave and you'll live."

"I don't think you'll kill me."

"You'd be wrong." She added a bit of steel to her voice. She'd not have a problem slitting his throat like a pig's. He was bad.

Zebada swallowed hard, causing a bit of blood to drip on the blade.

"Let's keep moving." Calli spoke in a firm voice. "I don't like just sitting here."

"Right." Beka's knife went back to its hidden sheath and she patted Zebada's back. "You just behave, alright?"

Zebada didn't answer as the horses started to walk.

"You mentioned Keth. Did you…?"

"Pierce is fine."

Calli seemed to relax a little then shook her head. "Thank you, but that wasn't what I meant. Did you talk with Keth about your mother?"

"So you did know I was his niece. I thought you might have with some of the comments that you made."

"With you looking like you do? Of course I did. And your father confirmed it."

"I'd notice the mousiness. Is it only our family?"

With a glance at Zebada, Calli nodded, "The royal family."

"I heard most of them died in the 'war' with Rennon."

"Only from the direct line. Your ancestry is from a sideline."

"But why don't my brothers look like me if it's

inherited?"

"I don't know." Calli shrugged. "However, Keth's father looked like his Eldanian mother, but as you saw his children all had the look."

"But why only the royal family?"

"If you believe the Priests than it's because they have dragon's blood in them."

Both looked down at Zebada as he spoke.

"That why you all attacked the Borderlands, Zebada?" Calli gave the question a sarcastic twist. "Cause it was ruled by tainted blood?"

"So say the Priests," Zebada replied.

"But we all know that's not true. The King of Rennon wanted the Borderlands. Rich land makes a rich king, does it not?"

"How should I know what that King wanted, Messenger Penn?"

"Men always want what isn't theirs," Calli told him. "Witness yourself."

"I only want what was stolen from the Church."

"Stolen goods should be returned to its original owner, don't you think?" Beka spoke in an amused voice. "Not those that stole it in the first place."

"It was given into the care of the Church," Zebada said with what could be dignity.

"But it belongs to the dragon, yes?" Beka paused, then continued when Zebada didn't answer. "So the dragon should have a say in what to do with it."

"I'd like to see that." Calli laughed. "The Priests talking to a dragon."

Ahead of them coming over a hill was a group of riders. Beka pulled her horse to a stop, Calli a second behind her. Both women kept their eyes on the three riders as they came closer.

By the feel of the tendril in her head Beka knew one of the riders was Hawk. Probably the one on the daggit which was no doubt Warchild.

The other two turned out to be Keth and Pierce. Pierce halted his horse alongside Calli's and pulled her into his arms. Beka didn't see any more because she was pulled from her own horse by Hawk.

He pulled her close and buried his face in her hair.

# CHAPTER VIII

**"I**'m fine, Hawk," she told him, patting his chest. She could feel tremors go through him as he tightened his arms, causing a shiver to go down her own spine. "Thanks for the rescue."

Keth cleared his throat. "Sorry to interrupt but we need to be heading back before they get organized again."

Beka laughed, pulling away from Hawk. "I doubt they'll be coming after us, will they, Hawk?"

"Very unlikely."

"Hawk? I thought that guard…"

Hawk's glittering eyes met Calli's. "You've already met me twice, Messenger."

Calli's eyes widened. "Panas."

"I am Hawk," he told her. "I have no other name."

"I'd still feel better if we left this place." Keth leaned over and gathered the rope to the horse carrying Zebada. "May I ask who this is and why he's here?"

"You need to take very good care of him. He's very important to the Priests of Rennon."

"Who do you think I am, Messenger Penn?" Zebada asked.

"Prince Sabra of Rennon," Calli replied before looking at Keth. "Part of the information you sent me to get was about him."

"Well, well." Keth looked at Zebada. "What do you have to say for yourself?"

"My name is Zebada."

"Right," Keth said, slapping his thigh with the rope. "Whatever you want to call yourself, you're coming with us."

"Wait." Hawk held up his hand as the others turned to leave. He stared at Zebada for a moment and Beka felt him scan him before he spoke again. "He's been mind-twisted."

"What?" Everyone but Beka turned to look at Zebada.

"Hawk?" Beka gave a questioning lilt to his name.

"Someone has messed around with his mind and reinforced it with torture."

"What do you mean exactly?" Keth asked Hawk.

"When he showed what you humans call 'the softer emotions' he was beaten or whipped and was emotionally abused."

"You got all that from your scan?" Beka tilted her head inquisitively.

"The fear of punishment was forefront in his mind and it was linked to the rest." Hawk paused. "What would happen if a low level empath with no shields was raised by a projective empath who only projected negative emotions like paranoia and aggression?"

"Would you allow me to sit?" Zebada spoke as if they had not been talking about him. "This is a bit painful."

"I think not. I have a feeling you'd try to gallop off so for now you'll just have to suffer." Keth obviously decided that ignoring this was a good idea until they got back to Yagos because he turned his horse and headed back the way he had come. "You all coming?"

"We going to take the horses?" Calli settled against Pierce, just as obviously not wanting to ride bareback to Yagos.

"Of course." Pierce was the one to answer as he grabbed for the ropes, careful not to jar Calli. "We can always use them."

Hawk allowed Beka to get situated before pulling her tight against him. He didn't seem to want her out of his reach. The three of them brought up the rear of their procession as they all followed Keth and his prisoner.

Beka relaxed into Hawk's body and just allowed her mind to drift. After a bit Beka noticed that Calli kept looking back at them. She kneed Warchild, causing him to move until he was even with Pierce and Calli's horse. "What's the matter, Mistress?"

"What did I say to call me?" Calli raised an eyebrow.

"Calli." Beka bobbed her head. "Now what is it?"

"I just can't get my head around him." Calli nodded toward Hawk. "The guard, the dragon."

"How I juggled all three?" Hawk paused as Calli nodded. "Dragons are not human."

Pierce snorted.

Calli mocked punched Pierce, then turned her attention back to Hawk. "What do you mean?"

"Once on this Steed it required only minimum effort to remain on, so I used the rest of my mind to take over the guard."

"But you showed up in true form not long after the guard fell."

"That was a projection." Hawk looked a little sheepish. "I'm not quite that big."

"A projection?" Calli paused. "But the horses?"

"I projected fear at them."

"So you're not nearby?" Beka asked, a bit curious.

"I'm in the mountains near Yagos."

"That's a little evasive," Beka noted.

Hawk shrugged but didn't comment.

"How far are we from Yagos?" Calli asked.

"These are the beginnings of the foothills to the east." Pierce was the one who answered. "We're headed to Loris."

"Loris?"

"It's built like Yagos at the edge of the foothills and mountains," Calli told Beka. "There's also a trail leading to Yagos. I've heard of it but never been."

"The wagon took it," Pierce broke in. "We weren't looking there at first."

Beka felt frustration and anger coming from Hawk at Pierce's words. "I gather you felt me being taken?"

"You just vanished," Hawk told her. "I knew you were still alive but 'you' were gone."

"I remember them giving me a dose of Coren, though I was still groggy from what ever was on that rag."

"The drug kept you unconscious but I could feel you again and we followed the link."

"I've been remiss in not thanking you." Calli said. "I know you could have just rescued Beka and left me to my fate."

Pierce opened his mouth, but Calli touched his lips and shook her head silently.

"Like that would have happened." Beka snorted. "I would not have left you there."

Hawk gave Calli a nod of acknowledgment but did not comment.

"We going to stop in Loris?"

"Just long enough to pick up the mule and supplies we left earlier this morning." Pierce told Beka. "Hawk told us we were close so we headed out without them."

"What about Zebada?" Beka gestured at him. "He can't go the rest of the way like that."

"Not consciously." Hawk paused. "I can send him into a deep sleep, and he can travel safely that way."

"That's probably the only way he won't try to

escape." Pierce sighed. "We'll discuss it with Keth when we get to Loris."

A track appeared ahead and they urged the mounts to it, following it toward the mountains in the distance. It was obviously a wagon trail and well used. Like with Yagos they followed it up a hill and looked into a valley spread below. The village though was only half the size of Yagos.

Keth stopped at the top of the hill and turned to look at Pierce as the others joined him. "Why don't you and Calli get the mule while the rest of us head toward Yagos. You can catch up to us later."

"He can get rid of the other horse as well," Hawk said as he slid off Warchild. "I'll keep up with the mounts."

"Alright." Keth glanced at Beka who shrugged before looking at Zebada. "I heard what you said earlier and think it's a good idea. We can't afford for him to escape."

"Now just a-" Zebada broke off as Hawk grabbed his chin and made him look into his eyes.

"Sleep."

Zebada went limp and Hawk closed the blank staring eyes before letting his head drop.

"Will that last until Yagos?"

"I'll have to wake him," Hawk told Keth.

"Good." Keth turned his attention back to the others. "I'll stop at the way station tonight. That should give you time to catch up."

Calli slid off Pierce's horse and slung herself on the back of one of the other horses while Pierce nodded to Keth.

"Be careful." Beka didn't like that they were

separating but knew it was best. After all they couldn't take Zebada into town. "This close to the camp there might be other spies."

"Which makes me glad these horses have neither saddles or brands," Pierce told her. "And the tack is generic enough. We shouldn't have problems."

"That's why I'm sending both of you." Keth gave them a stern look. "No dawdling."

"Yes, sir." Pierce gave him a mock salute.

"Get going, you jester."

Pierce and Callie kneed their mounts and headed down the hill into the valley. After watching for a bit Keth turned his horse and led the others along a side track.

"You said we're east of Yagos." Beka moved Warchild up until he was alongside Keth's mount. She noticed Hawk stayed next to Zebada's horse.

" A little over three days by wagon," Keth agreed. "Once we got on your trail with the horses we caught up fast."

"I only remember them dosing me once with Corin."

"They probably gave you pure Corin instead of the tea when you were unconscious." Keth paused. "Are you alright? I've been remiss in asking that."

"I had only been there a little over an hour before Hawk showed up."

"He gave us no warning. Just slumped over, though he still didn't fall off."

"I felt her awaken through the bond." Hawk spoke up, though he remained by Zebada.

"I thought you were already 'out of body'." Beka glanced back with a raised eyebrow.

"I left only enough awareness in this body to ride while I immersed myself in the link. After I felt you awaken, I slid into the guard's mind. Controlling two bodies was taxing so I withdraw a little more from this one. The little brother felt this and helped keep this body in saddle."

"Little brother?"

"I think he means Warchild," Beka told Keth.

"The projection was easier, so I returned half of my awareness to this body."

"Which is when you changed our direction again after leaving the road." Keth nodded. "With Zebada after the Gem we can bet the King knows it's been found."

"It's been lost for decades if what Calli's said is true, so why the concentrated effort now?"

"We've been getting reports that the King's been looking unwell. Perhaps he thinks it will cure him-- keep him alive longer."

"Or he's heard the prophecy," Beka added.

"Perhaps. Either way he'll send someone to replace Zebada in the hunt."

"If Zebada is Prince Sabra, then the King will be sending more than that." Beka glanced at the sleeping prince. "Though if he's the torturer..."

"Zebada is his possession either way and he's not the kind to let others take what's his." Keth shook his head. "Jax's sister is a mind-healer. Once we get back I'll have her check him out."

They rode silently for a while, each sunk in their own thoughts. Beka wasn't sure what Keth was thinking about but she was going over the stories her mother had told her.

A lot of the stories had been about the Borderlands and dragons, but a few of them had been about the Kings of Rennon, about their cruelty to their people. After one such story her father had drawn her mother away and they had had an argument.

The story had been about the King poisoning his Queen after she gave him an heir. Beka wondered if it had been about the current King.

Single trees had graced the land around them, but now a copse of trees appeared ahead of them. A small cabin with a lean-to was set just within and Beka guessed this was the way station Keth had mentioned earlier as he headed straight for it.

"The Foresters set this up for travelers to use in emergencies." Keth pulled his horse up in front of the lean-to and dismounted. "There's a rougher shelter in a grove nearer Yagos."

Beka slid off Warchild's back and moved to help Keth settle the mounts in the lean-to. "What do you want to do with Zebada?"

"I'll take him inside," Hawk answered before Keth could. He slung the unconscious man over his shoulder and disappeared around the cabin's corner.

"We'll get a few hours sleep after Pierce and Calli show up, then head out before dawn," Keth told her as they moved to follow Hawk. "We should be back to Yagos day after tomorrow if we keep a steady pace."

Hawk had left the door open and they stepped inside, Beka pausing to glance around. It was a typical one room set-up with a private privy; bunk beds around the perimeter with a fireplace in the rear wall next to a door. A large table sat in the center of the room with several mismatched chairs. The beds had blankets folded at their foot.

Hawk had laid Zebada on one of the bunks and was now setting up the fireplace.

"Not bad." Beka moved to the table and sat down. "I suppose we have to wait to eat until Pierce gets here?"

"Unless you want trail mix." Keth confirmed as he pulled out a small bag from his clothing. "There's more in the saddlebags."

"I'm hungry enough." Beka held out her hand and accepted the bag from Keth. Trail mix was jerked meat covered with honey and nuts. It didn't look like much but tasted good and gave you energy. "I don't see a pump or ware."

"Both are in the privy area." Keth gestured to the door in the rear wall, causing Hawk to get up from the fireplace and go in there. "It's a large privy area since it was the original way station."

"Oh?" Beka took a bite off the small strip of trail mix.

"The Foresters have been revamping their way stations over the past ten years."

"Why?"

Keth shrugged.

Hawk brought Beka a glass of water, then sat beside her at the table.

Beka yawned, then sighed. "I don't know which I'm more of--tired or hungry."

"Go ahead and rest. I'll keep a look out for the others." Keth gestured to a set of bunks. "We got awhile to wait."

"I agree." Hawk stood and held out his hand to her. "Come."

"All right." She laid the rest of the trail mix on the table and took his hand, allowing him to draw her up. "I'm too tired to argue."

Hawk guided her to a bunk and she stretched out with a sigh. He sat on the floor next to her and closed his eyes, seeming to go straight to sleep sitting upright.

Closing her own eyes, she relaxed into the mattress. For the first time since she had left her father's inn she felt completely safe.

# Chapter IX

The evening of the next day found all of them at the way station near Yagos. They had kept to a fast trot all day and had made good time. Pierce and Calli had shown up at dusk the night before and after eating they had all slept until just before dawn. The pace of the ride had kept talking to a minimum and allowed each to get some thinking done.

This way station was little more than an A frame with a roof out to one side to shelter the mounts. After settling the mounts, they headed into the building with Hawk carrying Zebada over a shoulder.

Inside were two double beds, a fireplace, a pump, and a door leading to the rough privy.

Definitely no creature comforts here Beka thought.

Hawk laid Zebada on the floor near the fireplace while Pierce set the bag of supplies nearby and Keth started a fire. Once the fire was started all of them sat on the floor around the fireplace.

"We'll be at Yagos tomorrow," Keth told the others. "We have to decide what exactly to tell the others and what to do with Zebada."

"You said you were going to let Jax's sister look at him." Beka raised an eyebrow.

"We have to figure out what to do with him after that, whether or not she can help him."

"As to rescuing us, just tell the others Hawk's contacts helped to locate us and Hawk got us away," Calli said. "Just tell them you can't reveal anything else."

"The Council knows who Hawk is, Calli." Keth paused, glancing at Hawk. "They just can't tell anyone else."

"Pierce told me what happened while we were in Loris. Serves Jax right." Calli huffed. "Any way you can still tell them what I said. They can repeat that to their people."

"True enough. But that still doesn't tell us what to do with Zebada."

"After Jax's sister looks at him we can talk with him once we have all the facts." Hawk spoke into the sudden silence.

Before anyone else could speak, the door was flung open and a cloaked figure stepped inside. The figure pushed down the hood to revel a middle-aged blonde.

"Jeni!" Keth stood. "What are you doing here?"

"An army is headed for the Scobee Pass," the woman told him.

"What!" Both Pierce and Keth yelled.

"A runner showed up this morning." Jeni closed the door and moved farther into the room. "Yesterday evening troops started to gather below Scobee Pass."

"Zebada must of had a far-speaker in his camp," Pierce said.

"This complicates things." Keth glanced over to the sleeping form of Zebada then looked back to Jeni. "We need your professional opinion."

Jeni moved to Zebada and squatted. "Who is he?"

"He calls himself Zebada, but Calli thinks he's Prince Sabra."

Her head jerked and Jeni looked at him in shock. "What?"

"That's not the worst of it." Keth paused. "Hawk thinks he's been mind-twisted, mentally abused."

"Your manners are slipping, Keth." Jeni looked at Hawk. "I'm Jeni Wey."

"Dylan Hawk, bodyguard." Hawk inclined his head to her. "I have a bit of talent and put him to sleep. If you need him awake..."

"I can do an initial scan with him asleep." She gave a small wave of her hand before turning her attention back to Zebada. A second later, she stood and turned toward the group. "Well, Hawk is correct; this man has been emotionally and physically abused which has warped him somewhat."

"Can you help him?" Beka asked as the others

were absorbing the news.

"I think so." Jeni paused. "He is conflicted so there is still a chance, but he must want to change for any healing to work."

"Then let's wake him and ask him." Beka looked at Keth with a raised eyebrow.

Keth sighed.

Hawk moved to Zebada and touched his forehead. "Awake."

Zebada jerked awake and scrabbled away from Hawk. "What are you?"

Hawk stood and stepped back but didn't speak as Jeni stepped closer.

"My name is Jeni. I'm a mind-healer."

Zebada's eyes flickered to her.

"I would like to help you."

"No one can help me." The words were soft, barely audible.

"I believe I can."

"My father won't like it." Again the words were barely audible. "He'll kill us both."

"He'll have to find you first," Keth told him.

"He always finds me."

"Do you wish to at least try?" Jeni asked him.

Zebada stared at her for a long time, then nodded.

"Excellent. We'll start tomorrow." She squatted and touched his forehead, causing him to slump unconscious. Gently, she laid him out on the floor before standing. "He is very conflicted."

"Pierce and Calli will stay with you until I can send someone." Keth sent a glance to Pierce who nodded.

"I'd prefer if Pierce stayed for a while."

Keth raised his eyebrow.

"His mental presence is--soothing to me. " A faint blush touched Jeni's cheeks. "And he doesn't project."

Calli laughed at the look on her husband's face.

"I don't have any designs on him," Jeni hurriedly explained.

"Oh, I know," Calli assured her.

Keth cleared his throat.

"You can send a guard. Just be sure he's steady and used to Healers."

"What about the rest of us?" Beka asked. "We still going to Yagos in the morning?"

"For a bit, then I have to head toward the Pass with some men."

"Isn't the Queen going to send her army?"

"Who are soldiers. But my men are scouts."

"You're going to need Messengers and runners." Beka raised an eyebrow.

Keth looked over to Calli.

"Don't look at me, boy. She's your niece. Besides she's right."

"I know." Keth sighed.

"Dinner will be ready soon." Jeni spoke up from the fireplace. She had moved there while the others were talking and had dug through the supply bag. A pot was hung over the fire and she was stirring it. "Soup and what's left of your journey bread. Make sure your guard brings supplies; this is pitiful."

"We've been on the road," Keth told her. "By the way how did you know we were here?"

"I didn't. I planned to meditate and try to mind-speak to you if I could."

"You're not a far-speaker?"

"No, but I do have a longer range than most mind-speakers." Jeni shrugged. "I thought it at least a good try."

"Did the runner say anything else?"

"Just that there's rumors that the dragon has awakened. Nothing solid as of yet."

Keth sent a glance to Hawk before turning his attention back to Jeni. "What are reactions to that tidbit?"

"People are worried about who the bonded is, of course. But most of what I heard in Yagos was positive."

"Are people associating the gathering army with the awakening of the dragon?"

"I don't know." Jeni shook her head. "Both the gathering and awakening are new so there hasn't been much time to assimilate."

"Mmmm." Keth sat on the floor and stared at the wood boards.

"I know your father taught you how to use that knife of yours," Calli said. "But did he teach you any other fighting skills?"

"Just some basic self-defense moves." Or so her father called what he had his cousin teach her and the boys. "Our cousin Jimi actually did the teaching. He used a pitchfork instead of a staff and taught us some hand-to-hand."

"He the cousin that went into the Guard?"

"He's a sergeant now."

"You should learn the basics of the sword as well as the bow if you're going to be amongst the

Army."

Keth raised his head at this.

"I'm going with Keth to the Pass. I'm not staying behind," Beka warned her.

"I think a crossbow would be best." Keth paused. "It's easy to learn and fits better on a saddle than a bow. However, I do agree she needs to learn how to at least block swords. But she can learn all this on the way to the Pass if that is her desire."

"It is." She was good with a knife, but she knew she would need more training, at least in self-defense, if not of the offensive weapons.

"Then that is settled." Keth nodded. "Unless Hawk has something to add?"

"It is always advantageous to be able to protect one's self, though no one will get close enough to hurt her."

Beka rolled her eyes while the others smiled.

"Dinner is ready." Jeni sat a plate of journey bread on the floor before Keth. "The cups and bowls are by the fireplace. Serve yourselves."

Everyone moved to the pot and grabbed either a bowl or cup, dipping it in. Once they got the soup they went back to the middle of the floor and sat down. Keth ignored the bread but the others took a bit and began eating.

A knock startled everyone and with a glance at Keth, Pierce went to the door. With another glance, he opened the door to reveal two older Foresters. "We were just eating. Would you care for some soup?"

"We have just finished our own meal, thank you." The older of the two spoke. "We wish to have speech with your leader."

"Please enter in peace." Keth made a gesture for them to come in.

Pierce stepped aside and the two Foresters left their leafy cloaks by the door, revealing their dark tunics and trousers. The door closed behind them and Pierce remained standing there while the Foresters joined the others on the floor.

"What is it you wish to discuss?" Keth took a sip of his soup.

"An army is gathering at Scobee Pass and the dragon has awakened." The older Forester spoke. "The Prophecy is unfolding."

"I really got to hear this prophecy," Beka muttered.

"What has this to do with us?" Keth raised an eyebrow.

"The Final Battle is coming and we wish to be a part of it. We know you will be heading to the Pass and we wish to give allegiance to you."

Keth's eyes widened in surprise. "Why me?"

Both Foresters glanced at each other before the elder spoke. "You're the Hale."

"The King of Kings?" Keth shook his head. "How do you get that?"

"A prophecy of our own."

"I'm no king."

"That's neither here nor there. What will be, will be." The elder Forester took out a bag from his tunic and shook it onto his palm. A bronze medallion with a chain lay there for a second before he handed it to Keth. "This will speak of our allegiance."

Keth accepted the medallion, studying the design of an oak leaf and a sword before he slipped it over his head. "I accept this in service of the Queen."

"Accept it however you like, but it is to you our allegiance goes." Both Foresters stood. "We will join you at the Pass."

Pierce opened the door for them, then closed it behind the Foresters as they left.

"First thing when we get to Yagos, you're getting me a copy of that prophecy." Beka spoke into the quiet that had settled after the door closed. "Ma's story said the evil man tried to steal the Gem and the dragon appeared to fry him after he kidnapped the girl. Nothing about king of kings or anything else."

"Our grandfather wrote that tale for a five-year-old," Keth told her. "He expanded it a bit when we were older but nothing specific. I promised you a copy and you shall have one."

"There's no need to wait either." Jeni rummaged around in her cloak and pulled out a small wrinkled scroll. "This is a rendered copy of the original."

"Yes." Beka accepted the scroll gingerly. Though a copy she could tell it was old so she carefully unrolled it to read.

"The dragon's Gem will be lost for a hundred and one years and will be brought forth by a girl rich in humble origins, causing the dragon to awake. An evil man will seek to steal the gem and an army will gather at the Pass named for the horse general while the king of kings joins with the warrior queen. Blood will flow and evil will seem to have the upper hand until the girl is brought before the evil man. At her word the dragon will smote all the evil before her with cleansing fire.”

“That’s a literal copy of the Eldanian translation of the words,” Keth said. “But some of the original words can have two different meanings. Aules can mean steal, but it can also mean possess, so it can read ‘to possess the Gem’ and smote has multiple meanings. Each word would add a different context.”

“Many scholars tried to decipher the original right after it was proclaimed but it was soon pushed aside by more daily concerns,” Jeni added. “Then it became legend.”

“What concerns me is that the Foresters think I’m the king of kings mentioned.”

“The Foresters have a lot of prophecies,” Jeni told him. “I wouldn’t take what they say seriously. Just be grateful for the extra man-power.”

“You’re right.” Keth sighed and stood. “Beka and I had best get some sleep if we’re going to leave before dawn in the morning. You mind if we take the beds tonight?”

The other three shook their heads as Hawk and Beka got to their feet.

Thoughts of sharing a bed with Hawk caused an odd tingle to shoot through Beka. Warmth. Hawk’s presence always made her feel safe, and the idea of him holding her while she slept made her feel even safer.

“Then we’ll bid you goodnight,” Keth continued as he headed for one bed and Hawk and Beka for the other.

# CHAPTER X

Dawn seemed to come early. Beka awakened to an empty bed with Keth standing over her with a mug of tea. She had felt oddly disappointed. Though there was not sexual attraction between her and Hawk, he made her feel safe and she sought his warmth. Both emotionally and physically.

The three of them had eaten some trail mix and gotten on the road within an hour of her awakening. Only Calli had seen them off; Jeni and Pierce had remained inside with Zebada. Beka had taken Warchild at Calli's insistence, but Hawk had refused a mount, saying he would keep up. They didn't argue with him.

Beka absently noticed that he was actually

'flying' or 'levitating', not running, and soon turned her attention to keeping Warchild at Keth's mare's heels.

Five hours of hard silent riding saw them at the hill above Yagos.

Keth pulled up at the summit and gestured for the other two to join him.

"Something wrong?" she asked. She hadn't seen anything and Hawk wasn't tense.

"I'm going to be busy for a while when we get down there, so I wanted to talk to you now." Keth paused. "I want you to prepare the stables as I'm going to have some of my scouts put their mounts there tonight and stay at the inn. We're going to leave within two hours of the meeting."

"The stable can hold up to twenty-five," she commented.

"And the inn can hold ten," Keth said. "I don't know how many will answer the call. We have to leave some to guard the town and keep up appearances."

"After we've got the stables set, we'll come to the inn. Jak can handle the stables and it will make him feel like he's helping."

Keth frowned but nodded. "I agree. Otherwise he'd be hanging around the inn, getting into trouble. Tad will no doubt be helping with the supplies."

"Better to keep them occupied than to leave them to their own devices."

"Hmm, true." Keth kneed his horse and they all started down the trail toward Yagos. "And with you and Hawk next to me there won't be any questions about your allegiances."

"At least not aloud," Hawk said.

"Yeah." Keth bobbed his head. "But with you coming with us they'll see."

"True," Hawk acknowledged.

"Milord." A guard appeared before them.

"Ro," Keth acknowledged the guard as they pulled their mounts to a stop.

"Word's gone out," the guard told them. "The Council is assembling a meeting."

"Good."

The guard bobbled his head then disappeared again.

Keth kneed his horse again and they headed down the trail again. A few minutes later they came to the edge of town and a man was waiting to take their mounts. As soon as they dismounted the man led the mounts away and Keth and Beka, with Hawk beside her, went their separate ways.

Beka found Jak already at the stables pitching hay. Several small bales of it had already been done. She gestured for Jak to come to her.

"It was all right that I did this, wasn't it?" he asked, obviously nervous.

"Yes. I was just going to ask if you can handle the stables while Hawk and I stay with Keth during the meeting. There's going to be a lot of people and horses."

"Theo said she'd help me."

"So you think you can handle it?"

"Oh, yes." Jak was all smiles.

"Good." She patted his shoulder, then with Hawk turned and headed toward Ken's Inn. They made the walk in silence. Just inside the door, they paused.

Keth was sitting at the large table with the Council. Beka and Hawk grabbed chairs and set them on either side of Keth before sitting down in them. Wills merely raised an eyebrow, but Jax scooted her chair further away.

"Jak taking care of the stables?" Keth asked.

"Yes." Beka nodded.

Jax frowned.

"Something wrong, Jax?" Keth asked her.

"No, just didn't think you'd involve Jak or Tad in this mess."

"They're old enough to have a say." Keth shrugged, then looked toward the door as the townsfolk started to wander in. "Besides better to give them something to do than let them get into trouble."

Jax continued to frown.

The inn filled up pretty fast. Every chair was taken and there was a lot of people standing along the walls.

Keth stood and everyone quieted down. "Ladies and gentlemen, it is time. A Rennon army is gathering and we must do our duty to the Queen who succored us."

Before Keth could say anything else, Jak busts into the room. "Uncle Keth! Someone tried to kidnap Theo!"

"What?!"

Jens enters the inn behind Jak.

"What's going on, Jens?" Keth asked.

"Why don't you ask Jax?" Jens said. "The kidnappers told us all about 'the plan'"

"If you had just been at the stables," Jax told Beka as she pushed herself away from the table. "You and that-thing."

"What are you saying, Jax?" Keth asked.

Jax tensed her jaw and didn't answer.

"She hired two drifters from Segar's Tavern to kidnap Beka. But they mistook Theo for her and tried to take her. Luckily I was there."

Whispers and mutters spread among the people around them.

"Jax, why?"

She tightened her lips and kept quiet.

"She may be quiet now but she wasn't in front of the drifters." Jens paused. "They said she ranted and raved about Beka being a deceiver."

"I told you she's my niece." Keth looked at Jax. "Nothing more."

"She's playing upon your grief!" Jax exploded. "Your sister ran away and was no doubt killed soon after. This girl is playing upon your uncertainty about her fate."

"Why would you think that?"

"Because that's what she would do." Beka spoke up. "It's what she's been doing probably since your wife died. She wants you no matter what it takes."

Hawk nodded.

"Did she help Zebada's men when they kidnapped you?" Keth glanced at Beka.

"No use lying," Hawk told Jax. "I can read it in your mind. Had I known earlier…No matter. Keth will take care of you now."

"Good to know you're not infallible," Jax spat. "And have some control over your murderous tendencies."

"You will not provoke me." Hawk spoke calmly though his eyes glittered.

Jax tensed even further.

"Stev, Garn, escort Jax to the holding area." The two men he named stepped forward and dragged Jax from the tavern before he turned his attention to Jens. "Theo?"

"At the stable with three guards." Jens waved his hand. "She's fine."

Keth sighed in relief, then looked at Jak. "You'd best get back there yourself, Jak."

"Yes, sir." The boy looked disappointed but he left.

"This can't divert us from our main objective. We need to get our gear together and head toward the Pass," Keth told the people around him. "The Queen needs us."

"I'll take care of things here," Jens said.

Keth gave him a nod, then glanced around at the others. "We leave in two hours."

Exclamations and gasps answered him.

"No reason to stick around and we will meet others on the way," Keth told them.

Grunts and nods went through the people before they all filed out of the inn, leaving Keth, Beka, Hawk and Jens alone..

Falling into his chair, Keth dropped his head into his hands. "Strife."

"I got you gear, Beka, and left it at the stable." Jens looked at Beka. "Ken's making you and my brother food pouches. You both should make his deadline in plenty of time."

"Thank you." Beka gave Jens a nod before turning to her other uncle. "Keth, you are not responsible for her actions. She made her own choices."

"I know." Keth sighed and raised his head. "You should get back to the stables and make plans with Jak for your absence. I'm sure he'd be glad to watch it while we are gone."

"No doubt about that." Beka paused. She didn't want to leave him like this.

"I'll stay a bit, Beka," Jens said. "I'll get it through his thick head that he can't control everything."

Beka nodded and stood as did Hawk. "We'll be ready." She nodded to both uncles, then headed out the door with Hawk.

They walked toward the stables in silence for a while, then, "Do you need anything? We never asked you," she asked Hawk.

"I am fine."

"Will your dragon self go to the Pass?"

"Perhaps."

Jak met them just outside the stables and led them inside. Half the stalls were full and one held Warchild. "Uncle Jens brought him with your gear."

"Where is that gear?" she asked him.

"There." He pointed to the stall next to Warchild. "I was packing it up and getting it ready when the kidnappers came. When I came back I finished so it's ready to go."

"Thank you." She paused but decided to be straight forward. "What do you think about keeping an eye on the stables while Hawk and I are gone?"

Jak's face lit-up. "Yes!"

Beka smiled at his enthusiasm. "It's a big responsibility."

"I know." The glow didn't fade a bit.

She nodded, then headed toward her gear, Hawk following. "Let's see what we got."

The two hours passed quickly after that. Beka and Hawk helped Jak saddle all the mounts as they were called for, then it was time for them to join the group. They took their leave of Jak and then led Warchild toward the others.

Keth turned his horse so he was facing the group. "Thank you all for coming. I don't know what the future holds but you will all be remembered by those that still stand at the end."

A ragged cheer greeted his words.

He turned his horse back around and with a motion of his hand, he started forward, leading them toward the distant pass where all their fates now rested.

# CHAPTER XI

The group traveled the next two days pretty much in silence, their thoughts heavy with what awaited them. Beka and Hawk helped every evening with the horses but left the morning saddling to the riders. It was slow going as they had to accommodate the two wagons that traveled with them, but they still made good time for all that.

On the morning of the third day, they spotted the Queen's army. Keth sent a messenger right away, and the messenger returned with a request for him to see the Queen.

"Thank you, Quinn. You may go." Keth dismissed the messenger, then looked at Beka and Hawk who were standing next to him. "Will you come with me?"

"You expect treachery?" Hawk asked.

"Not treachery, per se. But it's better safe than sorry."

Hawk looked at Beka. "You're apprehensive."

"I just got a bad feeling about this," Beka said. "The leaders all in one place, away from their usual protection."

"Another reason I want you to come." Keth glanced around at the resting people. "I'm going to leave Dan Oles in charge. Everyone respects him and he's an ex-soldier. If we don't return…Well, he'll take care of things."

"You'll return," Beka said.

"Enough doom and gloom," Keth said. "How bout it?"

"We'll go." Beka glanced at Hawk who nodded.

Keth nodded and went over to an older man nearby. He spoke with him for a few minutes, then came back to them. "Ready?"

Beka and Hawk nodded.

The three of them went over to the horses and Keth and Beka swung onto their already saddled mounts. Hawk trotted alongside them as they headed toward the Queen's army.

Four knights and the queen meet them halfway between the two groups. The knights were in full armor while the black-haired queen was dressed in a long purple robe and trousers with white trim. She and Keth moved forward so they were a little ways in front of their people.

"Your Highness." Keth bowed his head.

"Lord Shallan. What means this?" The queen gestured toward his group. "Are you here to take the leavings or to fight?"

"And which side?" came from one of the knights.

"We are here to fight for the Queen who gave us refuge," Keth said.

"Then you and yours are welcome," the Queen said.

"Thank you, your Highness." Keth bowed his head again.

"Join me." The Queen turned her mount toward her army.

"As you will." Keth stood up in his stirrups and waved toward his group before urging his mount to the side of the Queen's. He and the Queen with one knight following headed toward the queen's army.

"Your people will join at the end," said one of the remaining knights. "We will share our provisions with you when we make camp tonight."

"Thank you, Sir," Beka said.

The knights both turned their mounts and headed back to their army while Beka and Hawk returned to their group. Dan Oles immediately met them.

"We're to join at the end of the army," Beka told him. "They'll share some provisions tonight. Keth is talking with the Queen. That's all we know."

"We'll probably make camp in the valley near the pass by noon today," Dan commented. "Depending on the pace."

Everyone around them were mounting their horses and getting into a formation.

"They have supply wagons so it won't be a fast pace," Beka said. "And they'd probably would like some fresh meat for tonight."

"Good idea. I'll have a couple of the boys hunt before tonight." Dan nodded. He mounted his own horse, then the three of them moved to the head of the formation. With a wave, he led the way toward the queen's army.

They slotted in behind the army but before the supply wagons. Two of the scouts broke off and joined the dregs behind the supply wagons to ensure no surprises. The ride was accomplished in silence. As soon as the Queen's army stopped, the rebel scouts broke out of formation and set up their own camp a little ways away from the main army.

The valley had a forked river and the main army set up near one of the forks while Keth's group made camp near a treeline off to the side of both the river and the road.

Keth returned to them on foot after both camps were set up. Hawk, Dan and Beka stood with him at the edge of their camp.

"I have to return for supper, and I'll be spending the nights with one of the Queen's knights," he told them. "The opposing army is on the other side of the Pass. As long as they stay there the Queen will let them be, but the second they set foot on the Pass she will attack them. Her knights think there may be some of the army on this side of the pass already, just in hiding, so set guards tonight and send out watchers tomorrow."

"Right." Dan nodded. "You gonna be with the Queen during any fighting?."

"Yeah. Seems the knights don't trust me out of their sight." He tilted his head toward the other camp where a knight stood watching. "The Queen seems okay though."

"She likes you," Hawk said.

Keth raised an eyebrow then smiled when Hawk nodded.

A horn sounded two notes and Keth spun around to look toward the knight who made a come-on gesture. Keth hurried away while Beka looked to Hawk.

"I think the other army's on the move," Hawk said.

A man came up to Dan and said, "The Rennon are heading for the pass. I think they're going to try and take it."

Dan and the man hurried away toward the other men.

"Hawk?"

"That would be the sound strategy. Whoever owns the pass, controls access to both sides."

A Forester came up to them. "There are men coming through the trees."

"Rennon?"

"They appear to be," the forester told her.

"Thank you," she told him before hurrying off with Hawk to find Dan. Dan was with a group of men saddling mounts and they rushed up to him. "There are enemy in the woods heading this way."

"How many?"

"I don't know."

"Mannie, take half the men and go see about this."

A young dark-haired man nodded and motioned for Hawk and Beka to lead the way. The Forester was waiting at the edge of the wood for them and when Beka and Hawk showed up with over thirty men, he shook his head but led them into the forest.

The forester stopped suddenly and Hawk drew his axes. Men came out of the trees and started to attack the group. Beka kept her back to a tree and watched as the others fought. Hawk whirled around as he fought different men, moving farther away from her.

Suddenly a rag covered her mouth and nose and she slumped, overwhelmed.by the drug saturating the cloth.

She was still conscious but she couldn't think or feel anything. Hands dragged her away from the tree and she was flung over a shoulder. The clothes looked familiar but she couldn't place them and she just drifted along as the man carried her away from the fighting. Three more times the rag was applied as the man moved through the forest to where a horse was waiting. The man slung her over the horse, then got up behind her, kicking the horse into a trot.

Beka knew she'd be sore later, but she felt nothing now as she bounced against the horse. The man applied the rag again and Beka drifted along until the horse stopped. She was thrown over the man's shoulder again and he spoke but she didn't understand the words. However, the voice was familiar and she struggled to recall his name but the drug still held her. The man carried her into a tent and allowed her to slip from his shoulders onto something soft.

She finally got a glimpse of his face.

Zebada!

No sound came out of her mouth when she screamed that name, but the recognition was obvious on her face.

# CHAPTER XII

"Yes, Zebada," came a voice from the doorway of the tent. A Rennon man in gold robes entered the tent and joined Zebada by the bed Beka lay on. "So you are the one who caused me all that trouble with my Jewel."

Beka tried to talk but all that came out was a hoarse croak.

"The drug dulls the mind, body, and emotions," the king said. "It was developed to try to control dragons and their companions. The more it's used the stronger it is."

Beka tried to talk again but stopped and frowned in frustration.

With his right hand, the king reached inside his robe and pulled out a sheathed dagger. The metal hilt was shaped like the head of a dragon and the dagger itself was curved like a crescent moon. He handed it to Zebada.

"What is this?" Zebada asked.

"A zigga. You will need it to cut out the dragon heart."

"You want me to cut out her heart," Zebada said.

"Yes, and I'll take it from there."

Zebada stared at the dagger for a long moment, then moved onto the bed. He unsheathed the dagger and knelt beside Beka.

The king moved closer and leaned over the bed.

With a quick movement, Zebada shoved the dagger into the king's chest and jerked it upward before pulling the knife out and pushing him away. The king fell to the ground and Zebada slid off the bed to kneel by him.

Blood bubbled up from the king's mouth as he tried to speak.

"I did escape but not before the healer broke your control," Zebada told the king. "I am still what you made me, but I am no longer your puppet."

The king gurgled.

Zebada sat staring at the king for a few minutes until he died, then turned and raised his head to look at Beka.

She tried to speak again.

He stood and continued to look at her, the dagger held loosely in his hand, dripping.

Their eyes met and held.

Something flickered in Zebada's eyes and he blinked before looking toward the king's body. "I won't be like him, but I cannot change what he made me."

Beka cleared her throat and he looked back at her.

"The drug will wear off soon," he told her. "As much as I've enjoyed this, I think it'd be best if I wasn't here when it does."

She moved her mouth slowly so he could read her lips.

"Your friends are fine." He moved to the entrance and called, "Guard."

A man stepped in and Zebada grabbed him, jerking the dagger across his throat. Zebada dropped the man and leaned out the entrance before ducking his head back in. He slipped the dagger into his clothes, then with a glance at Beka, disappeared out the entrance.

Beka tensed, but still couldn't move so she relaxed onto the bed. Her emotions were still numb, but she was starting to think more clearly. She heard shouting outside and tensed again, but still couldn't move.

There was the sound of booted feet hitting the ground outside then two men burst in. The one man stopped just inside while the other man went to kneel by the king. He checked the king, then looked at the other man and shook his head. Both men then looked at Beka.

Gathering her mental resources, she screamed, "Hawk!" in her mind.

Chaos erupted suddenly.

Both men drew their weapons and ran toward each other. They began fighting one another while equine screams echoed from outside and Beka could hear fighting out there as well. A dragon the size of a cat flew into the tent and landed on the bed, his eyes on the two fighting men. The men stopped fighting and turned toward the bed, even as more men appeared at the entrance.

Warmth spread through her body and Beka twitched. She tensed and found she could move so she sat up, her eyes flickering between the dragon and the men.

The word 'dragon' echoed through the men facing Beka. Weapons were drawn but lowered as they all stared at Beka and the dragon. Beka knew the dragon was Hawk but she didn't know whether he was really there or if it was an illusion.

Hawk carefully climbed up to her left shoulder where he settled, his eyes never leaving the men as his claws gripped her just as carefully. *Slowly stand up*, came his voice in her mind.

Beka scooted to the edge of the bed and slid her feet to the ground. Keeping her own eyes on the men, she pushed off the bed and stood.

The men moved aside, making a clear path through the entrance.

*Go ahead.*

Moving at a slow pace, Beka approached the men. She knew one of them would be stupid and try something when she got to the entrance so she was prepared when one of the men tried to grab her.

He drew back a bloodied hand and Beka was standing just outside the tent with her knife in her hand and Hawk hovering above her. They stood like that for a moment, then Beka sheathed her knife and turned away, Hawk still hovering above her as she walked away. The other men shifted but remained where they were.

*I scared the horses away.*

"Of course you did." Beka sighed. Which meant she'd have to walk to wherever the camp was.

*Keth is not too far away*

"What?"

*When you were taken he gathered some men and followed. Your kidnapper left an obvious trail*

"It was Zebada." She stopped at the edge of the camp. "How close is Keth?"

A horn sounded in the camp and she made a gesture. "You don't have to answer."

Amusement flashed through her mind from him.

"Just lead me toward them," she told him.

He flew off toward the left and she followed, dodging tents and men until they came to where both forces stood facing each other. Keth's people were on mounts while the greater force of Rennon were spread out before them on foot. Another horn sounded but sounded further away.

"That would be the Queen's men," Keth told the Rennon soldiers."They were a bit behind us."

Beka moved to reveal herself and walked over to join Keth. The Rennon cleared the way when they caught sight of Hawk.

"Beka, are you all right?" Keth asked her.

"Just a little bruised from the ride here over a saddle," she told him as she turned to face the Rennon soldiers. Hawk settled on her shoulder. "I didn't think you'd realized I was gone."

"My men came and got me after the fight and Hawk passed out."

*The drug broke the connection and I returned to my true body.*

Beka gave a nod of acknowledgement. "I was drugged by Zebada when he took me."

"Zebada?!"

"Yes, Zebada or more precisely Prince Sabra," came Zebada's voice as his horse pushed its way through the Rennon soldiers to face Keth. "As I told Beka, your friends are fine. I got away once they broke the latent mental hold Father had on me. I am still as he made me but I am me."

"Where is the king?" Keth asked.

"Dead." Zebada paused. "Though I am his only legal offspring, there are other heirs. I will have to go back to the capital and lay claim. I ask that you allow the soldiers to return without hassle to our lands."

"I'll advise the Queen of your words. That's all I can do."

Zebada glanced over at Beka and Hawk then looked at Keth. "You can do more than that, King of Kings."

Keth sputtered, then gestured toward the rest of the camp. "*If* they leave on foot right now with nothing but what they carry."

"All I can ask," Zebada said as he turned his horse around. He gave Keth a nod, then spurred his horse and rode away.

The Rennon soldiers started moving after him.

.A Forester appeared at the head of Keth's horse. "We will see them safely back to their lands."

"Thank you."

The forester nodded and disappeared after the

soldiers.

"What are you going to tell the Queen?" asked one of his men. "She will probably want to detain at least the Prince."

"Our relationship with Rennon will be better off if we just let them return unmolested."

"That was not for you to decide," came a voice from their right.

The Queen and three of her knight sat on horses there. One of the knights was a little ahead of the queen and was staring at Keth with his visor up.

Keth turned his horse to face them. "I did what was best for both sides."

"That was not for you to decide," repeated the knight.

"Who better than the ones most affected by the king of Rennon's greed?" Beka asked as she moved to stand beside Keth's horse. She felt Hawk on her shoulder but didn't see him. "The king did not take away your kingdom, enslave your people, yet you think you and your Queen have the right to judge, to decide fate?"

"You dare speak…"

Hawk let out a low growl, making all the horses move nervously, and the knight stopped talking as he tried to control his suddenly wild horse.

"Someone should." An elderly Forester moved to the other side of Keth's horse and stood facing the Queen and her knights. "King Keth has every right to decide Rennon's fate."

"King! He dares…"

"That is enough, Clois," the Queen said. "By blood, he is royal."

"Your Highness…"

"Just because his kingdom is occupied by a hostile force does not make him any less a royal," the Queen told her knight. "I would still be Queen even if Rennon had won the battle earlier."

The knight bowed his head.

"What would you have happen here, Lord Shallen?" she asked Keth.

"Allow the people themselves to leave. Your men can loot the camp."

"And you?"

"I have what I came for." Keth gestured to Beka. "I care nothing for anything in the camp."

"That's not exactly what I meant," the Queen said.

Keth's eyes softened. "That is up to you, Milady."

"Let it be as he said," the Queen told her knights. "I expect to see you tonight at my tent, Lord Shallen."

"As you wish, Milady." Keth bowed his head.

The Queen turned her horse and led her knights away.

Keth relaxed and motioned for his followers to go before looking down at the Forester. "Thank you for your support, sir."

A nod, then the forester left as well, leaving Keth with Beka and the invisible Hawk.

Keth slid his foot out of the stirrup and reached out a hand. Beka took advantage of both and Keth pulled her on to his mount while Hawk took to the air. Keth nudged his horse into a walk. "I had Hawk's body taken to my tent."

*Good*

"Where are we?" Beka asked, glancing around. She had been semi-conscious after all and had lost track of where she was.

"In the foothills east of Scobee Pass. There's a few small passes along this area. I'm thinking the king was going to catch the Queen's army between two wedges of his."

"He was also here for me. He was going to have Zebada cut out my heart and jewel."

*He could only do that with a zigga.*

"What?!" Keth exclaimed.

"The king gave Zebada a special dagger." Beka felt Hawk run through her memory of the tent.

*The creator only made three zigga. They were thought to be destroyed. He will be a danger to us as long as he has it.*

"Zebada killed his father. With the dagger," she added.

*And he was thinking about killing you.*

"I hope he was telling the truth about Jeni, Pierce, and Calli being okay." Keth said.

"He didn't have any reason to lie to me when he told me the same thing earlier," she told him. She figured it was a peace offering of sorts.

Keth grunted.

They rode the rest of the way in silence as Hawk flew in wide circles high above them. Beka slid off the horse before Keth dismounted and turned over the horse to one of his men. Both of them watched the dot that was Hawk fly away.

"You can use my tent tonight," Keth said as they started to walk through the camp toward that tent.

"That's right. You'll be with the Queen." Beka raised an eyebrow.

"I don't know, Beka. I like her."

"But you're unsure about her feelings." Beka wasn't.

"Yes." He paused as they stopped before a big square tent. "I'll leave you here."

Beka watched him walk away then moved to the tent entrance. Opening the flap, she stepped inside and ran into a solid form. Arms caught her and she looked up into Hawk's human eyes. "Hawk."

"Come, let's get you settled. The drug plus the abuse. You should rest." He led her over to a plush mattress with bedding and pushed her down on it before joining her. "Do you need me to make you sleep?"

"Yes, my mind's spinning."

He rolled her on her side, spooning up behind her, and she felt herself slide into darkness.

# CHAPTER XIII

Beka and Hawk were eating breakfast when Keth entered the mess tent. He grabbed a cup of hot chi and joined them. His eyes were bright and alert even though he looked tired.

"Well?" Beka asked.

"I'm going back with the Queen. Sort of an ambassador. With the King dead, I'm now considered the ruler of the Borderlands again, though still in exile until the situation with Rennon is resolved."

"That's good, isn't it?"

"Yes." He paused as he took a sip of chi. "Though not so good for you. It means the Council is in charge of Yagos."

"And there might be some hard feelings about

Jax," Beka finished.

Keth nodded.

"I've been thinking about deeding the stables to Jak. That is if the rest of the family is staying in Yagos."

"I believe they will. It's been home for a long time. And I don't want to--strain the Queen's generosity."

Beka nodded. "So I thought Hawk and I could travel a bit."

Keth raised an eyebrow.

"I've always wanted to see the Borderlands."

"Ah. Start anew."

"Yes." She nodded again.

"That may be wise," he said with a thoughtful look. "Yagos will probably be streaming with people after we get back to the Palace."

"Hawk and I don't need that kind of notoriety."

"I would send you with coin."

Hawk held up his left hand and an uncut diamond appeared between his fingers.

Keth bowed his head.

"As you can see, that is taken care of," Hawk said.

"You are going to leave today then?" Keth asked.

"I think it would be best, don't you?" Beka asked. "Before the rumors spread even further."

"You've heard them?"

"Hawk has. And none of them come near the truth."

"A clean break then," Keth said.

"Yes." Beka handed him a folded sheet of paper.

"This deeds the stable to Jak when he comes of age and names Wills as administrator until then."

"Wills is a good choice." Keth accepted the paper. "I'll give it to Oles to give to him. You've been busy this morning."

"I had a good sleep and plenty of time to think this morning while helping with the horses." Her mind had been clear this morning and she had made good use of it.

"You sure this is what you want to do?"

"With the rumors and what happened with Jax…" She shrugged. "It'd be better if we didn't return to Yagos."

"The Queen would like to speak with you about what happened in the tent."

"I think it would be best that the exact details be a mystery," Hawk said.

A knight entered the mess tent with two men of arms. They paused inside then headed towards Keth. Keth stood and faced them as they reached the table. The knight and Keth stared at each other for a while, then the knight gestured toward Beka. "The Queen requests her presence."

"Beka?" Keth asked.

"Now's a good as time as any." She and Hawk stood.

"Just you," the knight said.

"I go where she goes," Hawk said.

"Obviously not," the knight said. "I didn't see you when she was rescued."

"You didn't look hard enough," Hawk returned with a growl.

"He goes or I don't go." Beka laid a hand on

Hawk's arm as she looked at the knight.

The knight inclined his head and gestured for them to follow before heading toward the mess entrance. They trailed behind him as he led them through their camp and into the Queen's camp. He weaved in and around a bunch of tents until he stopped before a tent ten times the size of Keth's. The knight waved the guards aside and lifted the tent flap, gesturing for the others to enter.

Inside was a large room with smaller closed off areas leading off the main space. A small throne was at the far end with an oblong table in the center covered with papers and maps. It obviously doubled as an audience chamber and the war room.

On the throne the Queen sat in royal blue robes with some of her advisers and knights. She motioned for them all to come forward. When they were in front of her, she spoke to Beka. "You look better than you did yesterday."

"I feel better as well, your Majesty." And would rather not be here, she added silently.

"Can you tell us what happened in that tent?"

"Not much to tell. Zebada…Prince Sabra kidnapped me and took me there. His father came in and ordered him to kill me, but instead Prince Sabra killed his father. As soon as I could move I hightailed it out of there." Short and mostly the truth.

"There are reports of a small dragon," one of the advisers said.

Beka and Hawk both raised an eyebrow.

Keth shrugged.

"Why you?" another adviser asked.

Keth raised his eyebrow this time.

The Queen looked amused.

"Look, I don't know much. I was unconscious most of the time." She thought it best to nip this questioning in the bud.

"Do you remember anything they said?" a knight asked.

"Not really. The drug kept me confused."

"You can't tell us anything about your captivity?" the knight asked.

"Not much. Zebada…Prince Sabra, kept me unconscious and under the drug's influence until just before he killed his father."

"So Prince Sabra killed his father. You didn't have anything to do with it?" one of the advisers said.

"How could I? I couldn't move."

"We only have your word for that," another adviser said.

Hawk took a step forward but Beka laid her hand on his arm.

"Believe what you will," Beka told the adviser. "I told you what I know."

"Somehow I doubt that," that adviser said.

"I hope you're not suggesting…" Keth began angrily.

"He's not suggesting anything," the Queen said with a glare at the adviser. "Why don't you escort your niece back to your camp and come back later."

"As you wish, Milady," Keth said with a nod.

The three of them backed away, then turned and left the tent. They weaved through the camp until they came to their own camp and headed for the area with the mounts.

"I'm sorry, Beka."

"They need someone to blame." She made a dismissive gesture. "I was the only other person in the tent. Who's alive." And she wanted to keep it that way.

"And the Queen won't let them blame you," Hawk added quietly.

Keth's ears reddened.

"Milord," a familiar voice to them all said. Pierce and Calli stepped up to them.

"Calli," Beka said and went to hug the older woman. "You're all right."

Pierce and Keth clasped arms, then stepped back.

"When did you get here?" Keth asked Pierce.

"Just now," Pierce replied. "From Beka's greeting I gather you know of Zebada's escape."

"He snatched Beka," Keth told him. "But as you can see we got her back. The king's dead, Zebada killed him."

"Jeni thought he might."

Beka and Calli stepped back from each other and Calli nodded to Hawk.

"Where are you all going?" Calli asked.

Keth and Beka looked at each other, then Keth turned Pierce around. "Come with me," he told Pierce, leading the man away toward the mounts.

"Hawk and I are leaving." She figured honesty was the best policy with Calli.

"As in leaving to go back to Yagos or leaving, leaving?"

"Borderlands leaving," Beka told her.

"I'm suspecting that there's a story here."

"A convoluted one. And Zebada is in the middle of it"

"You don't have to leave."

"Yes, we do," Beka said. "The rumors have already started." She had seen the others looking and whispering.

"They'll die down."

"Not soon enough." Beka paused. She swallowed around the lump in her throat. "Thank you for everything you've done for me."

Calli stepped forward and pulled her into another hug.

Beka allowed herself to sink into the hug for a moment, then stepped back. "Next time you see Father tell him I am well and following my heart."

"Are you? Are you following your heart?"

"Yes. The Borderlands have called to me since Mother spoke of them. And now I have the chance to see it for myself."

"And the perfect tour guide." Calli glanced at Hawk.

Beka nodded.

Keth and Pierce came up to them leading Warchild.

"No…" Beka began. The lump in her throat got bigger.

"Yes," Pierce and Calli both said before Pierce continued. "You'll have need of him."

"More than me," Callie added.

"There's a bag of trail mix and the rest of our supplies," Pierce said. "Should be able to get you through a few days."

Beka moved over to them and gripped Pierce's

forearm in a warrior salute. After he returned the salute, she stepped back and swung up into Warchild's saddle. She gathered up the reins, then stared at each of them for a moment. This moment had to last her a long time. "Thank you all for everything."

"We will see each other again," Keth promised her.

"If that is our fate," she agreed.

"We make our own fate," Keth said. "So this is 'until we meet again'."

Beka inclined her head to him in acknowledgment, then turned the daggit and gave a nudge of her knees to get him to start walking. She didn't look back or to the side, but she knew they were watching her and that Hawk was striding beside Warchild. They passed through the Queen's camp next and approached the Pass. The guards waved them through and they continued on.

Once half way through the pass, Beka stopped and looked back at the camp. Pressure built behind her eyes.

"We will see them again," Hawk told her.

"Perhaps, but when?" Beka stared at the camp for a bit then urged Warchild on.

"Specifics I cannot give you," Hawk said. "But we will return."

She nodded.

According to her mother's stories dragons lived a long time. So a handful of years or even a decade was nothing to them but she hoped they would return before that many years passed. She pushed that worry aside and turned her attention forward.

This land had once been the Borderlands but had been occupied by Rennon troops since the invasion. Zebada would wish to establish his rule over Rennon before he turned his attention towards this land. Which would take years giving everyone breathing room.

Once on the other side of the pass, they skirted the nearly empty enemy camp and headed southeast toward the old capital. Warchild stretched his legs and Hawk trotted along side.

Perhaps they would meet some of Keth's spies and set up a better network, paving the way for Keth to lead a rebellion against Zebada. Or perhaps Zebada would make a treaty with Keth and let the Borderlands go once he establishes his rule over Rennon. Now that the king is gone, many possibilities were available.

"The old prophecy was wrong," she suddenly said.

"Depends on how you look at it," Hawk said. "Technically or literally."

"What do you mean?"

"Zebada is short for Zeb Ah Daia or Lizard of Fire. More commonly known as Dragon. Sabra means 'To Smite'. So technically a dragon smote the king."

"What about cleansing fire?"

"He's probably going to do that as soon as he's king. Getting rid of those who are strict followers of his father's. And the translation you saw was a literal translation from a literal translation. Soooo…technically, it came true."

Beka frowned.

"Is it really that important?"

She shook her head.

"Then let it go."

"I'm just worried that if that was wrong, then what about the king of kings bit."

"The way Keth and the Queen were looking at each other, that bit will come true. Though really it's already true."

"More technicalities?"

"Yes." He flashed her a smile. "You need not worry."

Beka sighed.

"Everything is as it should be."

"Even this." She gestured around them.

"That is why you're here, is it not?" Hawk asked her. "To set things into motion, to set things right? Or at least your version of right?"

She raised an eyebrow.

"We could have gone anywhere. You choose the Borderlands."

"True enough." She inclined her head then glanced at him. "Did you want to go somewhere else?"

"Wherest thou goes, I shall also," he told her.

"That really doesn't answer my question. Did you want to go somewhere else?"

"In a way it does answer your question. You are my--Kin."

"Kin?"

"That's the closest word in your language. The Creator made us so that we have a--check on our power. Someone to balance us."

"Wouldn't your mate do that?"

"No." Hawk shook his head. "We mate but we do not stay with them once the mating is done. It is just a biological impulse to continue our species. We were created as battle companions to our Kin."

"So one of the great scientists did create you from the legendary fire lizards?"

"Yes." Hawk nodded. "Which is why they are so rare now."

"I thought that was one more of Mother's tall tales."

"No."

"So you are all right with this?"

"Depends on what you mean by this?"

"Freeing the Borderlands from Rennon's grip," Beka told him.

"I figured that is what you had planned."

"Who better than a member of the royal family that has such protection as you?"

"What about all that about not liking notoriety?"

"I don't, but someone needs to work here while Zebada reassures his reign of Rennon itself. Keth can't do it and if any of the siblings do it, it might be taken the wrong way."

"Like they want to be the ruler."

"Right." She nodded.

"You seem to have it all thought out."

"As I told Keth, I had a plenty of time to think while we helped with the mounts," she told him. Consequences, contingency plans. She thought quite a bit on the road.

"It may take a long time and constant vigil to get where this land can stand on its own."

"It won't need to stand on its own."

Realization flickered to life in Hawk's eyes. "Keth knew what you planned."

"I'm sure it crossed his mind. But he will be sending Eldanian emissaries once he has an arrangement with the Queen."

"And by the time they reach the old Borderland capital you'll have paved the way for negotiations with the locals."

"Yes."

"You are definitely a descendant of kings," Hawk told her.

"I'm sure you mean that as a compliment, but diplomacy does not come easy for me as it does Keth. The prophecy gave me the thought. To be king of kings he has to be a king to begin with. For that the Borderlands needs to be completely free of Rennon rule. And to do that the people themselves must work toward it."

"Truly a descendant of kings."

Beka inclined her head.

Silence reined as Beka sunk into her thoughts of how to inspire rebellion against one king and support for another among a people who had been under the heel of occupation.

# EPILOGUE

*Beka rode slowly through the city, Hawk pacing patiently at her side. People came out of the one and two story buildings along the route she took, merging and following behind her. She was headed toward the temple district, not the large castle that loomed over the city. There she could address the people and perhaps be able to finish her speech before any Rennon soldiers still here could try to silence her.*

*She turned into Temple Road. The temples were built of stone and towered over the surrounding buildings by at least a story. Some had open courtyards while others were enclosed by stone walls. Halfway down the street was a three-story building with a large open courtyard and Beka stopped there. It was the temple of the All-Father.*

*Using her knees, Beka guided Warchild to the front steps and turned him to face the crowd. Hawk stood by her side and let his mind wander over the people gathering.*

*They had done this at every city they had come to. Finally they were at the end of the line. The capital.*

*Beka looked at Hawk and he nodded. And she began as she had at every city and town. "The King of Rennon is dead...Long live King Keth."*

# ABOUT THE AUTHOR

Tina Riffey always wanted to be a writer. She started with poetry in grade school and moved to stories by high school. Through a series of moves, she lost those earlier stories, but continued to write down story ideas through the years.

This is her sixth book but the first in the fallborn series. The fallborn series is about dragons and their companions. Each is set in a different world where dragons either exist or had existed and had or do change the world by that existence.

You can visit the author's main blog at Http://www.tinariffey.blogspot.com

The fallborn series is kept up to date at http://www.dragconicsidereal.blogspot.com

Tina lives in Southern Missouri with a bevy of feral cats.